The Tarahumara Crystal

The Tarahumara Crystal

Donald Taysom

NPI

Northwest Publishing, Inc.
Salt Lake City, Utah

NPI

The Tarahumara Crystal

All rights reserved.
Copyright © 1996 Northwest Publishing, Inc.

Reproduction in any manner, in whole or in part,
in English or in other languages, or otherwise
without written permission of the publisher is prohibited.

This is a work of fiction.
All characters and events portrayed in this book are fictional,
and any resemblance to real people or incidents is purely coincidental.

For information address: Northwest Publishing, Inc.
6906 South 300 West, Salt Lake City, Utah 84047

JC 1.19.95

PRINTING HISTORY
First Printing 1996

ISBN: 1-56901-659-3

NPI books are published by Northwest Publishing, Incorporated,
6906 South 300 West, Salt Lake City, Utah 84047.
The name "NPI" and the "NPI" logo are trademarks belonging to
Northwest Publishing, Incorporated.

PRINTED IN THE UNITED STATES OF AMERICA.
10 9 8 7 6 5 4 3 2 1

To Kim,
for being there, for reading, and for encouraging support.

chapter
one

The peculiar landing attitude of the Twin Otter made Clayton Kile uneasy, adding to his discomfort with the sudden and unwanted assignment into Baja. The last minute delivery of the briefcase, as he was boarding, still rankled his sense of precise planning. An erratic path, as the plane settled onto the tarmac, unnerved him even more. None of the eleven passengers noticed the sway of La Paz Tower or the traveling undulation of the runway. Neither were they aware of a widening fissure just below the pilot's line of sight.

As Kile was being assisted into the ambulance, he realized he'd experienced the slow-motion syndrome that sometimes occurs during accidents. He could not, however, recall sounds of the crash.

There was a brief examination as first aid was applied. That was when he again became aware of the obnoxious man in the aloha shirt, the mouthy one who owned a speed shop in Compton, the one he'd done his best to ignore on the flight from Tijuana.

It took some convincing to assure the doctor and the represetative from the airlines that the minor contusions and the abrasion on his cheek were the extent of his injuries. He refused to be x-rayed.

He was about to ask where he might find his one piece of luggage and the briefcase, when a young, well-uniformed officer appeared. "Your personal carry-on belongings, I believe, Mr. Kile." He spoke English with no trace of an accent. "Was anything checked?" he added.

"No, this is it, Officer...?"

"Montoya, sir, and I have one simple request. Would you open the combination lock on the briefcase? It has no identification and doing so would confirm ownership."

"Certainly, Officer." He placed it across his knees and adjusted the tumblers. "It contains confidential business papers that I would..."

"That is not a problem, Mr. Kile. I do not have to see the contents."

Kile raised the top enough to see his two files and some brochures. He swallowed slowly; there was much more underneath...money.

"Are you all right?" Montoya asked.

Before Clayton Kile could assimilate what he'd seen and come up with an answer, someone yelled in Spanish. Montoya excused himself and rushed toward the exit.

"Sure you're all right, buddy?" It was the speed shop man. "You look like a hound dog that's just been bred."

"What?" Kile looked up. "I'm sorry—preoccupied. Here on business, as I said. Have to make a call." He left, briefcase clutched against his chest, carrying the soft leather valise with his right hand. He was trying to recall what Trevis

Thayne said when he delivered the misplaced briefcase, something about—what was the word? *Mordida*—yes, that was it—a little cash for paving his way to the top man, the one who could make or break the deal on buying condo complexes in Cabo San Lucas. But this much? Clayton Kile's banking experience told him it was thousands.

Something was starting to form in his mind, a vague but complex hovering that didn't focus. He paused in the confusion of the terminal. He wanted a telephone or a place where he could open the briefcase again.

His attempts at concentration were shattered by the appearance of a slender, dark-haired woman forcing her way through the crowd, camera cases and bags swirling as weapons.

"Good god," he muttered. "This I do not need."

She looked directly at him and turned abruptly. She did not look pleased.

The movement of the floor startled an already confused and disoriented Clayton Kile. He knew it was an aftershock but could not help thinking it was some kind of confirmation of Meliss Courtland's presence. He exited the terminal and by sheer luck found refuge in a cab.

"You were on the plane when it shocked?" the driver asked, using a literal translation.

"Yes, but I'm not injured," Kile said, wanting to avoid the next question.

"You are here for the race, Señor?"

"The race?" He knew he should have said yes in order to conclude the interrogation.

"Señor, it is the Baja One Thousand. It is going right now and some of the leaders are more than halfway."

"Yes, of course." He remembered the annoying references by some of the passengers. "Is it crowded in La Paz?" Clayton wondered if there would be problems in getting to his appointment the following morning.

"Yes, it is very crowded. Do you have a reservation at your hotel choice?"

"I do, the Los Arcos. My employer has taken care of it."

"Ah, Señor, you are here for business then?" He looked at his passenger in the mirror. "Señor, are you not feeling well?"

Kile had again opened the briefcase. It was not only money; there were negotiable bonds underneath.

The hotel clerk's blank stare was a prelude to his statement. "I am sorry, Mr. Kile, but all of our rooms have been reserved for months. The Baja race, you understand."

"Try under Heritage Savings and Loan, they assured me it had been taken care of." He gave the names of Trevis Thayne, Clarence Dove, and two secretaries. The clerk shook his head, graciously made calls to other hotels, then said, "Perhaps if you tried in person?"

"Damn," he said, as he turned from the desk. "There's probably no appointment tomorrow either." Stunned, he tried to think. What are they doing to me? I need a place to sit down and sort this out, a quiet place, a room. No, a telephone call. That's it, I'll...

"Outside communication is impossible," he heard someone say as he worked his way through the roiling lobby crowd. "The race and now, of course, the earthquake."

The festering of questions that began at the airport had compounded into something far worse than a hovering cloud. Something is drastically wrong, he thought. Is it the venture that's being sabotaged or is it me? Perhaps both? I need a drink. No, it's much too early. Kile hardly noticed the next aftershock.

The main verandah, facing the sea, buzzed with conversation regarding the earthquake and the status of the One Thousand. The surprisingly mixed crowd, many of which were women, seemed unified by the subjects at hand. There was apparently little major damage and, other than people on his flight, no deaths or injuries. Seeing a vacant table at the far end, he made his way through the milling standees and arrived at the same time as two women.

"I'm sorry," he said. "I didn't know it was taken."

"We'll gladly share," said the dark-haired one wearing shorts.

The blonde smiled.

"It may cost you a round of drinks," said a third woman, as she came up behind him. They all laughed.

When the waiter returned, Kile paid. He had forced himself to endure the race talk. Downing his scotch, he stood to excuse himself. "Business, you know."

"We didn't mean it literally," said the blonde. "The round of drinks, I mean, but thanks anyway."

"Is there something bothering you?" asked the one in shorts. "You seem a little uptight."

"I was in the plane that cracked up on landing. I suppose I'm still a little dazed."

"In that case, the next round is on us. Waiter!"

"Well, well, buddy," a male voice said, "looks like you cornered the market already." It was the aloha-shirt mouth. "Can I join you?" He sat against the railing.

"I see you weren't as lucky as I," Clayton said, trying to be cordial.

"Oh, this," he said, nodding toward the sling on his left arm. "Not as bad as it looks. Damned sore, though. I see you haven't checked in yet. Room not ready?"

A siren sounded, rising to a faltering peak. "A little late," someone said. The sound receded.

"Excuse me," Clayton said, picking up his bag and the briefcase. "Have to check on my room."

He found the restroom, marked in three languages and a symbol, and entered.

"I will hold your bags for you, Señor," the attendant said. He didn't seem to fit. The starched linen jacket was even more of an incongruity.

"No thanks, I need them...to change."

"I can hold the one you are not needing."

"No," Kile said sternly and closed the door.

He opened the briefcase, lifted out a packet of fifties, and folded half of them into his pocket. If I was supposed to bribe my way into success, he thought, I'll see if I can payola my way into a room. He glanced, once again, at the negotiable securities, as good as gold anywhere in the world. That hovering thing, the vague cloud that had been trying to intrude, was now coming in clearly.

He closed the case, picked up the bag, and left. The attendant had disappeared. Missed his tip, Clayton thought as he again walked toward the desk.

"Yes, of course, the room is now ready, sir," the clerk said as he deftly pocketed the four fifties. "I will personally escort you." He called something in Spanish to a younger man seated in the back, then said, "This way, please."

Clayton Kile gave the man another two fifties and closed the door. He shook his head as he eyed the suite, the admonishments of the clerk still echoing. "This will be for no more than two days," he'd said, "and you may have to be moved quickly after the first day. You will also not be registered...is that a problem?"

chapter two

Rising rapidly from teller to loan officer, C. Andersen Kile, a name affected for the position, was very much at home in the preciseness of banking. His abrupt personality, however, did not lend itself well to public contact "on the floor," and he was consequently promoted laterally to comptrolling and auditing. This suited him even more, and he excelled. The C. Andersen thing was dropped, primarily because they began calling him Andy, and he again became known as Clayton.

Confidence in this field, the conservative but stylish attire, and his departmental acumen soon brought him an assistant vice presidency—and the attention of headhunters. The founders of Heritage Savings and Loan were looking specifically for this type of man.

Offered a substantial increase in salary, profit sharing, stock options, and a full vice presidency, Kile readily accepted.

After the clerk delivered his bottle of scotch, Kile attempted to relax and put things together. He had never been much of a drinker, limiting any cocktail party to two drinks, carefully nursed. Now, he was taking it neat—something he'd heard about the water—and it was working. He was beginning to see things, except for details, in startling clarity. It had been meticulously planned. Was I set up from the start, he wondered? No, he assured himself, it had to have been after the reorganization. "God!" he said. "Why didn't I see it?" He wondered how they opened his briefcase and how they got it through Mexican customs. He answered his own questions: Trevis Junior, for the first; he was good at that sort of thing. Surely bribery got it through customs unopened.

When he questioned some investments of the rapidly burgeoning company, he'd been told to take care of his department and leave ventures to the board of directors. When he brought up discrepancies in internal audits, it was suggested he was looking too deep for phantoms in a company experiencing phenomenal growth. Later they apologized and began using him to research and investigate potential expansions and ventures.

The latest was his concern about an enormous amount of cash coming in from what were supposed to be long-term investments. An oversight in bookkeeping, he was told.

Now, five years after he'd been hired, he was the sacrificial lamb. He was about to be slaughtered. All the other vagaries became clear: the bonuses, the exaggerated salaries, the perqs.

I wonder what the extradition procedure is, he thought, as he tried to layout some kind of action. They will want to catch me with all this, yet, at this point, I could easily clear myself...or could I? I doubt if they would rest on this setup alone. No, records will have been altered and there will be arrows of incrimination pointed directly at me.

Kile chuckled cynically as he remembered the clerk saying, "You will not be registered...is that a problem?" I wonder how much head start they will give me? How soon before they turn it over to the San Diego P. D.? No, it would be federal agencies. They have to have time to...no, I have to be caught with all this in my possession. I could just dump it somewhere. No, it's missing and I'm gone. Kile went on thinking of a myriad of things that could be rearranged to magnify the finger of guilt.

Then, as if there were some subconscious wish to replace this dilemma with another, he thought of the startling shock of seeing Meliss at the terminal. I wonder what she thought? That look—I'm sure she still despises me.

"Shit," he said, getting up to pour another scotch. "This isn't getting me anywhere. Got to think!" He set the glass down without drinking. With the fact of no reservation, there is probably no official to contact either. This whole thing was a scam to get me out of their hair and into some damned Mexican prison. By the time...what the hell am I thinking? Heritage is a paper house by now or soon will be. They wanted me out before the quarterly audit. I should have been picked up by now; that officer should have taken me in...why didn't he? There's one conclusion, the word is not yet out. The alleged losses have not been reported.

Clayton removed everything except the top layer from the briefcase and stuffed it into the leather bag. He stepped into the hallway and removed several newspapers from a table. Filling the case to its original level, he slid it under the divan. "I think I should eat," he told himself, "try phoning again, and then get the hell out of here."

Another stab of anxiety intruded as he took the last flight of stairs down to the lobby. It was much too quiet. The few people there and on the verandah seemed far different than the animated crowd he'd observed earlier.

"The dining room is closed," he was told. "It is usual to rest this time of day."

Clayton realized it was midafternoon. He also knew his earlier confidence was gone. Not wanting to ask questions at the desk, he walked onto the verandah. For the first time he noticed the view and the numerous boats anchored in the bay: motor craft and yachts of all kinds, some elegantly impressive.

A short walk took him to the central part of La Paz. The travel agency was closed until four. Two blocks later he found a sidewalk cafe that was open. The service was slow and he wasn't sure he got what he ordered, but he knew he should eat.

Maybe it was some kind of a joke, he thought later, as he sat on a palm-shaded bench bordering the beach. It was a feeble rationalization. He became angry again, but at his own stupidity for not recognizing the signs he could now clearly see. They had deliberately moved him when he got close to something, but they were convincing in their explanation. "You need experience in all departments," Thayne would say, implying promotion and his own branch.

"Damn," he muttered, embarrassed at his ego blindness.

"We have a flight to Los Mochis tomorrow morning," the woman at the travel agency said. "A small independent airline. Aeromexico has canceled all flights until runway damage is repaired."

"What time?"

"At nine. This evening's flight is filled. There is also the ferry, Mr...?"

"What sort of place is this Los Mochis?" Kile asked, evading the name query.

"A very nice town, but hardly a tourist thing. There is a great deal of fishing. There are buses to Culiacan, going south, and Mazatlan. You can also go north to Guaymas." She smiled. "If you are adventurous, there is a magnificent train ride up through the Sierra Madre from Los Mochis to Chihuahua. I can arrange accommodations for staying and visiting Copper Canyon. It is the Grand Canyon of Mexico."

"I'll think about that when I get to Los Mochis. Please book me for tomorrow's flight." He reached for his wallet, hoping there would be no request for identification or his tourist card.

This triggered another thought; if they had not planned this well in advance, how did they happen to have his card for him when he arrived at the Tijuana Airport? "Thank you for your help, Miss, or is it...?"

"Señora. Señora Valdez."

"I appreciate your information, Señora. Is there any possibility of a cancellation this evening?"

"Perhaps, but you would have a time problem in getting to the airport if there was a no-show. Some passengers go in our limo, others by their own car or taxi."

"I'll take that chance."

"Be here no later than five."

The verandah had come awake, and the gathering of race fans was building up for the evening cocktail hour. Edging through the lobby, he saw her again. Three men hovering in attendance did not surprise Clayton. She was an attractive woman. Independence and confidence, obviously gained in her rise as a free-lance photographer, made her even more fascinating. The black hair, tied in a bun, had lost none of its luster. The slender body of Meliss Cortland...Kile shook his head; he did not like remembering.

"Got checked in, I see," the familiar voice said. "How about joining me for a drink?"

"Yes, I did. Speed shop isn't it? L.A.?"

"Compton."

"I'll meet you in the bar. Just going to wash up."

"Name's Burt, in case you forgot."

"Fine, Burt, see you shortly." At least he changed that hideous aloha shirt. Spending time listening to racing engine specifications did not interest him, but acceptance seemed the easiest way out. Besides, he had to be back at the agency in fifteen minutes. He would apologize later if he didn't get the flight.

When he returned, at five-twenty, he was greeted on the verandah by Officer Montoya. "Ah, Mr. Kile. How are you feeling?"

"Tired, very tired," Kile said, hiding the sudden panic of possible arrest.

"Perhaps you need a drink?"

"Yes, I do. Would you join me? As soon as I take these to my room, I mean." He looked down at the briefcase and the bag.

"It is not my policy—a professional thing—to drink in uniform. And, of course, I am on duty. Perhaps another time."

I wonder what he knows, Clayton thought, if anything at all? If he does know something, why hasn't he arrested me?

"Yes, another time. Tomorrow evening?"

"If matters are concluded by then and things are again normal." He grinned slightly. "Things won't really be normal until the race is over and gone."

Clayton Kile, worried about "matters concluded," felt better with the expression of the last statement. "Are the racing people a problem?"

"Not generally, just rowdy at times. A pleasant good evening, Señor Kile."

"What the hell do I do now?" Clayton said to himself, as he dropped things to the floor and settled into the leather chair. I think he's suspicious, even if word hasn't come down. Can't hide, can't go anywhere until tomorrow, so might as well go into the crowd and act like an idiot. That is about the extent of my capability.

He washed, changed into what he referred to as his safari suit, then thought about the money and bonds. So what? It would be their loss, not mine...no, that's not it at all. Damn it, it belongs to the investors, the small depositors. He left things as before except for putting several packets and some of the bonds into large pockets of his jacket.

He signaled the attention of Burt and pointed to the verandah. Burt nodded and edged his way from the bar.

Once outside, Clayton looked for Montoya, but he was not in the area. She was. There was a brief recognition as their eyes met, but it passed quickly, as it had at the airport.

As he turned to greet the speed shop king a heavy aftershock rumbled through La Paz. Clayton Kile again wondered if it was symbolic.

chapter three

Four hundred kilometers to the northeast, where the Sierra Madre rises like the hump of a monstrous wild boar and gives great depths to the Barrancas De Cobre, lateral adjustments to tectonic movement created slides and fractures in the Great Copper Canyon.

The elderly shaman paused in his attempt to clear the bare face of a cliff where he was trapped when the centuries-old path disappeared. In his younger days it would have been a simple thing. It started to rain. Zabata knew he would have to find shelter; his bones did not like rain. He inched his way along the narrow confines toward what appeared to be a shadowed depression in the canyon wall. He hoped it would give some shelter.

He was not disappointed and entered the vertical crevice. He would rest until the water of heaven ceased. There had been no fear when Great Mother Earth shook her canyon, for he was a Tarahumara and he was a shaman. He slept.

Zabata had not meant to sleep through the night. Bright sun coming into the cave startled him. Nothing had bothered his sleep; he had not smelled animals, and unseen things were no problem, for he had often talked with spirits. He took deep breaths into his large lungs and rubbed circulation along the slender arms. As the sun moved farther into the cavern, he experienced a thrilling wonder; the walls were splashed with vivid colors. Never had he heard of a rainbow in any of the many retreats along the sides of Barranca De Cobre. Yet it was not truly a rainbow, for the colors were in segments and not curved.

With humble reverence, he watched the play of light, then followed the rays back from the walls to their source. In an upper fracture he saw sunlight change into colors as it emerged from a cluster of transparent crystals, very large crystals. This is truly a rewarding thing I am allowed to see, he thought, as the prismatic bending of light held his fascination.

He watched until the sun no longer reached the cluster. Still, there was enough light to see, and he approached the thing that caught and changed the sun. It was not an easy thing to reach that upper ledge, but he had to view this miracle. It was not wrong, for he should be allowed; he was a shaman. He marveled at the creation. Such crystals he had seen before, but never so large, or so many in one gathering. Some were as long as the span of his hand. He would count them another time, for he must hurry to the sacred place and leave word for the new speaker. The quorum must see this wonder, for it was truly a sign and somewhere, in the litany of previous shamans, he could recall legends of sacred light. Surely, he thought, I will be called for some service even though my chanting voice is gone.

• • •

Clayton Kile could not help watching Meliss as the trembler brought sudden silence to the lobby conversation. When it was over and staccato comments covering nervousness and fear rose, he knew he had to speak to her.

"Are you all right?" he asked, interrupting her conversation with two men. There was an impassive stare and silence. At least she's not glaring, he thought.

"What are you doing here, Clay?"

"I could ask the same question, but I am aware of your professional status in photography. Saw some of your work last year and…"

"What do you want?" she said, cutting him off.

"Nothing," Kile said. "Absolutely nothing, except to assure you I had no idea of your being here."

"Good! I accept that and the fact that our conversation is over." She turned and walked away, calling to the two men as she did, "I'll take that drink now."

Up in his room Kile sat alone, hating the fact that she still had an effect on him and regretting he had not been able to ignore her. Then, after sipping a single scotch, he convinced himself he was using the situation to cover his other problems and did not need that kind of complication.

Anxiety about the morning flight was aggravated as he eyed a DC-3 and its faded logo. He had not slept well, he had not eaten, and he still did not have a plan, other than getting out of La Paz before he was arrested. Surely he could make some telephone calls from Los Mochis. But, he thought, to whom?

Much concerned with the two hundred foot altitude of the plane as it skimmed across the Sea of Cortez, Clayton Kile paid no attention to the other six passengers. He was also hungry and getting irritable. He was not used to things being done without careful planning.

He shared a taxi into Los Mochis with three of the passengers, pleased that only platitudes were exchanged. "I am sorry, Señor," the driver said, in answer to Kile's question. "It is much too late for the morning train to Chihuahua. Do you wish a nice hotel?"

What are my choices? Kile thought, as they continued the drive into town, other than waiting for tomorrow's train or catching the bus to Mazatlan. He negated the latter—not an efficient way to travel.

Being advised he could not buy an advance ticket, Clayton made arrangements for the taxi driver to pick him up at five the next morning, assuring him of an extra tip if he was on time.

He checked in, had breakfast, and was escorted to his room which, to his pleasant surprise, was not in the hotel itself but a new one-story annex. Had he not been so preoccupied, he would have been amused by the stained-glass window in the bathroom.

"That was some good-looking gringo," a waitress said as she flirted with the desk clerk, "but he has much on his mind."

"Yes," the young man teased. "I do not think he wants a woman."

Their conversation was interrupted by a man who displayed an identification card and said, "Go back to your work, young woman, I wish private conversation with the clerk." Making sure there was no one else within hearing, the man continued, "What name did he use, the Norte Americano who just checked in?"

"He came in from La Paz on the morning..."

"I know that, I followed him from the airport. What name did he use?"

"Clay, Mr. John Clay," the clerk said, hurt that he hadn't been allowed to tell what he knew.

"Did he check anything into the hotel safe?"

"No, but he did have two items of luggage."

The man, who could have passed for any one of the many affluent farmers around Los Mochis, admonished the clerk about discussing his inquiry, then left. Later, he would report,

"He made no contact at the airport and none, so far, at the hotel. The taxi driver said he asked about the train to Chihuahua and is to be picked up tomorrow morning at five. There was no conversation between the suspect and the passengers in the taxi. He is using the name John Clay...I know, not very original. Still has the briefcase, but I can't guarantee that...Yes, I know, I will take care of it...yes, sir. I agree it is probably not to be a pickup on payment and that is unusual, if not most questionable. But, as you said, sir, the tip has been valid right down the line, so far."

Kile gave a great deal of thought to his dilemma, the outcome being that he should call an attorney, the one he was sure he could trust, and lay it all on the line. Then, he reasoned, he would have some basis for validating his story when he returned to San Diego. Contacting the desk, he made arrangements for the call. A few minutes later his phone rang.

"Your call to San Diego is ready, Mr. Clay," the clerk said.

"Hello?"

"Blanchard, Beck, and Murray Law Offices," a female voice said.

"Jim Murray, please."

"May I say who is calling?"

"John Clay," Kile said, masking his voice.

"One moment please." There was a pause of several seconds before a different voice came on line. "I am sorry, Mr. Murray is out of town for a few days. This is his secretary, may I help you, Mr. Clay?"

"Can he be reached? This is vitally important."

"He left no number but will be calling in. May I ask him to return your call?"

"No, that would be difficult. I'm traveling and not sure when I'll be reachable." He thanked her and said good-bye.

"Damn," he said, hanging up. "That takes care of that." I'll have an early dinner, he thought, stay away from the crowd, and get some sleep. Tomorrow night, if there is a flight out of Chihuahua, I'll go back. If not I'll catch the first one out the following day. I've got to chance it, and hope to God I don't get arrested between now and then.

There was another phone call to San Diego that finally got through from La Paz. It was to a private line at Heritage Savings and Loan. "Nothing's happened and he's gone across the bay...I don't know...sure, there's a plane at five...you want me to, hey, wait a minute, there could be a goddamn tap on this line...how much is in it?...You got a deal."

chapter
four

The shaman, Zabata, sat quietly with the council. There had been discussions of his find and they were now debating the question of it being the legendary Cave of Light.

"Did you not see other things?" one member of the group asked. "Things of sacred nature?"

"I was in great wonder," Zabata answered, "and my mind is old. Should we not see this together?"

"What is the legend," a young member asked, "that I have not been privileged to know?"

"Few know," said Callo, the new head shaman. "It has nothing to do with our present ways."

"I do know," said Zabata, "that it was the place of repose for Teporaca. There he received guidance from the spirit world."

"Yes," said Callo, "but he was betrayed by his own people, hanged for not repenting, and his body was filled with the Spanish arrows. He was left to rot as a warning."

"He swore at the Spanish soldiers as he was dying," added Zabata, "and he cursed the cowardice of the Tarahumara. It was not the last of revolts, nor the last of slavery in the mines. A great shaking of the Mother Mountains, after his death, hid the Cave of Light as punishment to the Tarahumara."

"We can send the *raramuri*," said the young one, "to all villages. There will be a great *tesquinada*."

"No," said the head shaman. "We will not use the runners; this will not be a carnival. It will be only for the initiated."

"Then a guardian must be appointed," said an elder, "for there are many who would use this to bring the," he switched from native tongue to Spanish, "gringo dollar."

"We shall be there in the morning," the shaman said. "And we shall see lights of the sacred cave. Zabata, return to this place, see that nothing is disturbed. Signal us the location with a fire before the sun tomorrow."

The newly opened fracture in the canyon wall was seen by another before the return of Zabata.

Tatla, one-time champion of the *raramuri* and later a respected member of the *matachine* dancers, had lost his coordination through a fall into the canyon. His mental capabilities were also diminished, and he wandered about the barranca with no apparent goal. He had his own terraces for food, but often forgot about them and then wondered why his corn, bean, and squash plants did not produce. He would sometimes sit near the narrow fields of a neighbor until he was invited to join the family for pinole, either dry or mixed. Tatla did not often go hungry.

He did not see the light show, for it was late in the day, nor did he see the wall paintings or the sacred artifacts. The cluster of crystals grabbed his attention, because he had seen the tourists buy such things when the train stopped at Barranca

Divisadero. These are grand, he thought, compared to small ones he'd seen before. One will bring a carrying bag of pesos, and I can buy gifts for those who have given me pinole. Something, a feeling perhaps, told him it was wrong. Yet he felt that just one would not matter.

Clayton Kile exited the cab and walked through the drizzle that followed the earlier storm. The crowd, milling around the station, disturbed him. Good god, he thought, these people can't all be going to Chihuahua. When he realized the group by the window was not buying tickets, he pushed his way forward. "Chihuahua, please, one...*uno*."

Seeing no available bench, he slumped against a wall leeward of the platform. He carried one piece of luggage, the briefcase having been emptied into the leather bag and then given to his driver. A VW bus splashed to a stop, and he saw Meliss Courtland slowly emerge. Why the dark glasses, he mused, maybe a rough night? I wonder when she got here? He thought of the men she'd been talking to in La Paz, angry at himself for feeling a tinge of envy. He assured himself he would not give her the satisfaction of putting him down again. She would have to be the one who spoke.

Involved in his thinking, he did not observe what might have been a familiar figure. Yet, he might not have recognized the man at all. Burt no longer had the persona of the speed king from Compton.

A group from Brownsville, Texas, occupied most of the first car, the one with the bar and grill, and welcomed Kile in chorus. One of them said, "Goddamn, boy, you look like you could be a Texan. Hey, Jed, you got a hat for this dude?"

"Jeff, you give him your own damn hat. I'll give him a drink."

Kile tried to look cordial and attempted a cowboy greeting of "Howdy." He wished he'd taken one of the other cars. He was not in a mood for this.

The Fiat train, while showing its age, operated efficiently

once underway, and Clayton grew comfortable with the now quiet Texans.

"Well, looky here at this filly coming in," Jeff said. "Come right on in, honey, we all got our partners, but there's a single dude just got on, and you all are welcome to party with us clear to Chihuahua."

Meliss shook her head slightly and said, "I'm sorry to disappoint you nice people, but I..." She took off her sunglasses. "See for yourself."

"Well now, sweetheart," Jed half-whispered, "we got a little ole Texas remedy for that. Gus," he said to the bartender-chef, "this here little lady is hurting, so fix her up with one of those drinks I taught you yesterday, and give her and this quiet dude anything they want, it's on the partners of the Double B and their wives."

Later, as Clayton emerged from the restroom, Meliss was waiting. "Look," he said. "I..."

"Oh shut up, Clay, I didn't plan this either. I wish to hell there was a compartment...I think I'm going to be sick."

"All I was going to say..."

"I know what you were going to say, that you weren't following me. I know that, and I'm sure as hell not following you. The staff photographer showed up, and I got bumped from shooting the finish. Now I'm supposed do a series on some stupid canyon and then go on to Chihuahua and do Pancho Villa's home and one of his widows. God, do you realize how old she'd have to be even if she was a child bride? Did you know his real name was Dorotea Arango?...What the hell did I drink? I'm babbling."

"Thanks for being decent," Kile said. "They are a nice group of people, they're having fun, and definitely do not need our...What is it—enmity, dislike?"

"Shut up, please, I don't need an analysis. Just what are you doing here, and in La Paz? That food smell—I am going to be sick. What's that asshole doing here?"

"Who?"

"He's gone now. He was looking from the other car. You know him, I saw you talking to him."

"Come on, we'll get you some air."

"Not back there, god-awful fumes from the engine. That's why I came forward."

It took not only *mordida*, but considerable persuasion to get into the front part of the engine. They accomplished it at the next stop.

Half an hour later, Meliss said, "It's over."

"You don't have to remind me, Miz Cortland."

"Clayton, stop being so stupidly defensive. I was referring to my being sick. God, I'm glad it's not hot. This moist air feels good. Thank you."

"Do you want to go back to the car at the next stop? There are a lot of tunnels ahead."

"Yes, I'll be ready."

chapter
five

An assembled council watched the false dawn disappear. Later, sun rays pierced through morning sky and flooded upper walls of Copper Canyon. Soon sunlight would penetrate a recently opened fissure.

"With torches we could search for the things spoken of," said one of the huddled group.

"No," said the shaman. "The lights will be watched first. It will be a sign that we should see what was left by those before us, those who refused to become slaves, those who were not cursed by Teporaca."

"Surely there will be graves and leg bone dust," said another.

"It is almost time, Speaker," said Zabata, as the sun

illuminated the acute angle of the cave ceiling.

There was silence as the first rays reached the crevice above them and speckled the inner wall with color. They waited.

"Something is wrong!" cried Zabata, as the less-than-spectacular show of rainbow light stabilized.

Later, when nothing more materialized, he scrambled along the wall to the cluster. There were grunts of disappointment as he examined the natural prisms of quartz. "One is no longer here," he said, voice faltering. "It has been broken off and taken."

Had Zabata not been held in high esteem, grumblings of doubt would have echoed through the cave.

"Search quickly," said an eager voice. "There may have been another shaking that did it."

When careful examination of the ledge was over, they looked about the sacred cavern, seeing objects hoped for.

"Yes," said the shaman. "This is truly the place of our ancestral priests." He held up the carved stick and let sunlight play on glittering stones. He then turned toward a wall where cult glyphs and paintings had not been seen for some three hundred years. There were bones, ceramics of great religious significance, and wondrous things to be examined and cherished.

"*Kwiri ba*," he said, greeting the spirits. Then, in the Uto-Aztecan root language, he began a prayer.

When they processioned out of the opening, after reaffirming Zabata as keeper, one remembered seeing the Lost One, the one whose mind is with the night, coming down from this area the afternoon before.

"Could he have found the sacred chamber?" said one.

"Surely he would not have damaged and taken…"

"How would he have known?" said a third, interrupting the second voice. "He is not much for thinking. Everyone knows that."

"Which direction was he going?" asked the shaman.

"I do not know," said the one who had seen him. "But we can talk to the old man who has his *galiki* and *dekochi* by the abandoned diggings."

"Send our *raramuri* to find where he walked," said the speaker shaman. "We must find him and discuss this."

At Heritage Savings and Loan, in a room they called their "Cone of Silence," sat three men. The CEO, Clarence Dove, quietly fought his nervousness. He was in that position because of his name, it rang up a certain reliability compatible with the image of Heritage, and due to the fact that he'd gone through bankruptcy several times and always came out financially secure. He was, in fact, the front man. The other two, a father and son team, were the movers and shakers of Heritage.

"I think we have to move now!" said Trevis Thayne. "The grand jury has been asking questions and wants an appointment with you, Dove, and the rest of us, eventually, I might add. We can't stall for long, as they do have the means of subpoena and we certainly do not want that. Not yet, anyway."

"What about our plan?"

"I am coming to that, Dove, just be patient. You have been through this sort of thing before, you know. The plan is not working out as designed. DEA didn't buy the informed source leak or there's a hang-up down the line somewhere. Maybe they're waiting for him to make a contact. I don't know."

"Then it's time to contact the local authorities and announce phase two." It was Trevis Thayne II, who would never fit, had no class, and hated being called Junior. But he was a technician.

"No, no, no! We can not bring criminal charges now."

"Why not, Trevis?" asked Dove. "It was in the original plan."

"For the simple reason…damn it, Dove, stop your ridiculous fidgeting. I want your attention, not a slobbering mumble...We are not sure where he is. He could be on his way back to San Diego. Our man informed me there was a call to a law firm here: Blanchard, Beck...and something. His informant, however, got called away from his eavesdropping, and we don't know what was said. It was a brief call, though."

"Dad, if the narc thing hasn't developed into anything and we can't file a criminal complaint yet, just what is the next move?"

"I told our man that if he could make sure Kile would not return...," Trevis Thayne looked squarely into the eyes of the others, "...the briefcase and its contents were his."

Dove gulped, the heavy undulations working his thin neck like an ostrich swallowing an orange.

"I don't like this, Trevis. I don't like it at all."

"What you like or don't like is of no concern, Clarence, and if you do anything to fuck this up, you will go to prison. I've seen to that, I guarantee it. You know how much is at stake here! Furthermore, I'm not about to give up a lifestyle I've found comfortable and secure. I will let you know when I hear from our man, but neither of you are in today... understand?"

chapter six

Meliss turned as she stepped up to enter the car and said, "This doesn't change anything, Clay, but I'm sure you know that." She continued into the corridor, not waiting for a response.

"A little presumptuous, aren't you?" Clayton muttered, as he watched her disappear into the crowd of Texans.

"Meliss, you little darlin'," Jed cried out as he stood up. "You just sit right here, by my Melody, while I fetch us a tad more hair of the dog."

"You've known him before, haven't you?" Jed's wife asked.

"Jed?" Meliss looked at her wide-eyed. "I swear, I...oh, you mean Clay. Yes, we knew each other years ago. A brief thing, lost contact. Still friends, though."

The Texas lady smiled and said, "Honey, you can't bullshit an old cowgirl, so why try? But if you don't want to talk about it, that's a different thing entirely. Ah, here's my Jed with our drinks."

When Clayton entered from the platform some thirty minutes later, Jed's call to join them was thwarted by his wife's boot to the shin and a coded smile.

The view became more spectacular as the train climbed into the Sierra Madre. Clouds dissipated, and dozens of waterfalls, caused by the recent storm, came into view. Each bridge and every tunnel caused cries of delight in the front car. Meliss found herself wondering where Clay had disappeared to. Ridiculous, she thought. He has been nice, though. God, if he hadn't taken things so seriously, if he hadn't...this is stupid. "I'll take that drink now, Jed."

The announcement that they would soon be stopping at the Barranca Divisadero and could view the magnificent Copper Canyon brought new yells of excitement. "I've been told," said one of the ladies, "it's bigger and more colorful than our own Grand Canyon."

"Well, now," said her husband. "I kind of doubt that."

"They say it's deeper," said someone else.

"My goodness," said one of the women as the train came to a stop, "they got a flea market all spread out right here."

Hardly a flea market, Meliss thought, as she looked at the myriad of artifacts and colorful stones. There were carvings of wood and bark, rustic jewelry, stone images, and small jars of stream-polished rocks.

On his way to the rock promontory that was carefully fenced with metal pipe, Kile caught sight of a lone Indian seated to the rear of the dozen or so purveyors of local goods. He was definitely not dressed for the benefit of the tourists and had only one object on the small blanket before him. It was a spectacular piece of quartz. Kile stopped, fascinated by the largest crystal he'd ever seen.

"He's trying to tell you of its powers," a man said to Kile, interrupting the combination of Spanish and Tarahumara. "It not only tells the future, according to him, but gives power of health, wisdom, and the ability to read the thoughts of others." The man laughed, then added, "It can increase a man's macho…no, that isn't quite right…his virility." The man laughed again.

"Thank you," Kile said. "Tell him thank you and that I'll consider it while I look at the canyon. You speak both Spanish and Tarahumara? I guess that's what it's called."

"Yes," said the man. "I'm in ranching, lumber, and a bit of mining. It's necessary to be multilingual. You are staying at one of the lodges?"

"No, I'm on my way to Chihuahua."

"Too bad, the evening views are even more inspiring. We'd better get on down there if we want to see anything. The stop here is only for a few minutes."

As they proceeded, the man added, "Is that not a nuisance, carrying your luggage?"

Kile looked at the valise, raised it to waist height, and said, "I travel light, and I suppose I am a bit paranoid about personal belongings."

From the train's rear car, the man known as Burt watched passengers move downtrail for observation platform access, then rushed forward through the coaches.

On his return, after the engine had signaled a second time, Clayton Kile could not resist the proffered crystal. "Sir," he said to the man accompanying him, "would you ask how much he wants?"

"You don't have time to bargain; we'll miss the train. Offer him some dollar bills, not more than five or six. He'll want to argue but will give it to you. Come, hurry, everyone's boarding."

Kile offered the handful of bills. There was hesitation on the part of the seller, and Kile handed him three more dollars. With the crystal in his free hand, he ran toward his coach.

Had he looked back after boarding, he would have seen two young Tarahumara men confronting the seller. Once seated, Kile carefully placed his purchase inside the bag, then chuckled to himself. The situation had, for a few minutes, given him freedom from his problems.

"That view must have done you some good," Melody said. "You look pert and proper."

"Thank you. It was spectacular, wasn't it?"

At the next stop, there was a van waiting and several people exited, including Meliss Cortland.

Three miles down the track the train slowed, blew its whistle several times, and stopped. A few minutes later it was announced that tremors and heavy rains had caused a series of slides. There would be a train coming up from Chihuahua. The railway official held up his hand at the surge of questions.

"Please," he said, "I will go over the options. You may wait here for the other train. There will be transportation beyond the slides for lodges there. This train will return to the last stop for persons wanting to try for accommodations there. It will then stay here for the transfer." He repeated in Spanish.

"When will the Chihuahua train arrive?" Jed asked.

"Late today, perhaps not before dawn." The conductor left, signaling the end of information.

"So much for the power of the crystal," Kile said, looking at the man who had been his interpreter, and joined him in the first coach.

"Are you missing some business of importance?"

"No. I was planning on flying to San Diego."

"We have talked, but I have not introduced myself. I am Señor Vargas."

"Clayton Kile." He offered his hand. He also realized it was the second time he'd used his real name. The Texans and everyone in the first car know, now Vargas. He was tired of charades and attempted disguises.

The man smiled as they shook hands. "Perhaps I can

suggest something worth considering. The group here will most likely go on to the newer hotel. Unless traveling there is of necessity, I would offer the hotel where the others got off as a more pleasant location. It has the superior views of the canyon. It could be a full day before the other train arrives, so why not be comfortable and enjoy the Sierra Madre?"

"Pardon my eavesdropping," Melody said. "But you appear to be local and we'll follow your judgment. You hear that, Jed?"

Jed nodded, as did the others.

"How far were you going today?" Kile asked as they reentered the car.

"To Creel. I have business there and will go on to my ranch."

An hour later they were delivered from the railway to the lodge. I wonder what her reaction will be, Clayton thought, as they entered the lobby. He realized he didn't care. Clayton Kile, chronically preoccupied, once again did not see the ubiquitous Burt bringing up the rear of the small group. He probably, as before, would not have recognized him anyway.

Dropping his bag to the floor, Kile tested the bed, found it acceptable, and attempted to relax. It didn't work.

I'm ready to find a cop of some kind and turn myself in, he mused, as he drifted into a light sleep, but for what?

Kile saw her when he came down for the evening meal. Not unusual, he thought, not at all strange, seeing her holding court in a small bar off the dining room. He did not blame the men in attendance. He was once part of a similar group but wanted more than a place in the chorus. When it was achieved, he couldn't handle it and an emotional disaster was imminent. Kile did not want to think about that period of his life. He shut it off.

He still admired the way she could unconsciously position her long legs. So sensual, without being cheaply provocative. Just as well I don't intrude, he decided, as he took an early seating for dinner.

How long he had slept he did not know, but screams from across the hall brought him to immediate and full consciousness. He glanced at his crystal, barely visible on the dresser, as though it held some answer. Plunging into the corridor, he listened, then threw his weight against the opposing door. It gave way in splinters, and he found himself facing the shadowy figure of a man.

The intruder whirled and jumped through the screen of the open window. Someone turned on lights, and Clayton Kile found himself standing in the room of Meliss Cortland. That he was clad in his shorts did not bother him. Even as other guests nervously assembled in the doorway, he was not embarrassed. This surprised him. Perhaps it was because the formidable woman with her overt confidence, a woman who had once been his emasculating nemesis, was now in a discomposed state of shock.

"Did he...?" Clayton paused. She looked so vulnerable. "I mean, are you all right?"

Meliss nodded.

"The *policía* will be here soon," someone from the hotel staff said. "Their station is not far."

"Was anything taken?" asked one of the tourists.

"This is a hell of a way to treat travelers," said another. "The management will hear about this. Did anyone go after the bastard?"

"He could not have gone far," said Señor Vargas, who had just entered. "It's a twenty-meter drop...to solid rock."

Jed's wife, comforting the badly shaken victim, said, "There, there, honey, it's all right now. Everything is okay."

As Kile turned to leave, Vargas reached out his hand and clasped Kile's arm. "Was it for rape or robbery?" he asked quietly.

Shrugging, Kile said, "Tell the officers I'll be in my room. Is there room service at this hour?"

"You need a drink," stated Señor Vargas. "I'll see to it."

Two things bothered Clayton Kile as he entered his room,

he had never responded so suddenly to any situation in his entire life, and his shoulder throbbed painfully.

It was the manager who arrived with a tray of ice, scotch, soda, and glasses. "Nothing like this has ever happened at this lodge, I assure you. The lady has been given a room next to the people from Texas, and I think one of their women will stay with her. I do not know how...Was the door in any damage when you...? I believe it was you who arrived first."

"No, it was solid and locked. I think it was locked....I'm not really sure. I'll pay for the door."

"That will not be at all necessary, Señor Kile, after all, you did go to her assistance. The hotel thanks you for that."

Three officers entered the room. "He is correct," the captain said. "Nothing like this has ever happened in any of our lodges at Copper Canyon. And, I believe, it could not have possibly been an attempt to molest the woman. That would not be the case. Do you know if the woman carried anything of exceptional value?"

"She's a professional photographer," Kile said. "Her cameras are expensive, I'm sure."

"Jewelry?" the captain asked.

"Nothing other than what she was wearing. Hell, I don't know. How should I? Ask her."

"We will when she feels better. The man is dead, you know."

"I thought as much, considering what Mr. Vargas said. That's one hell of a drop. Who was he?"

"He was not a thief, Señor Kile, he was one of the *raramuri*, a champion runner in fact. He did not even drink tesquina. Even during the celebrations."

Kile laughed. "Then what was he doing in that room?"

"That is what we are trying to find out. Did you have any contact with him? A scuffle of any kind?"

"No. I guess he panicked when I crashed through the door or he heard the others in the hallway."

"Had you ever seen him before?"

"Not that I'm aware of. I only saw his outline in the room. Couldn't possibly have recognized him."

One of the subordinate officers said something in Spanish. The captain commented, then turned to Kile as if to say something. There was an awkward silence. "Do you speak Spanish, Mr. Kile?"

"No."

"My local officer wonders if the runner might have entered the wrong room. He was dressed in the clothes of a kitchen helper."

There was a knock. "It's Vargas. May I come in?"

"Of course," Kile said, opening the door.

"We were just finishing our conversation," the captain said. "Do you know Mr. Kile, Señor Vargas?"

"We met on the train from Los Mochis, Captain Rosa. At Divisadero to be specific."

"I don't think there is anything else," the captain said in leaving. "But call our office when you leave. Will it be to Chihuahua?"

"Yes, and only to catch a plane to San Diego…or Tijuana."

"Sorry you have not had a pleasant stay. *Buena suerte*. Good Luck."

The three officers left, and Vargas closed the door.

"Do you want some company or can you sleep now?"

"What time is it?"

"About three."

"Have a drink with me."

"One drink. You look tired, then I'll leave."

They toasted, and Vargas said, "That is a fascinating crystal. I do not believe it has brought you much good fortune, though."

chapter
seven

Clayton Kile slept intermittently. Frustration with not being in charge of his life, confusion of recent events, and inner changes kept intruding. When he accepted that he could sleep no longer, he got up and walked to the window. The view of the canyon was so startling it short-circuited his attempts to analyze his feelings and his situation.

"I don't have a handle on any of this," he said after several minutes. "But I am not going to sit by and be the idiot victim.

He was just out of the shower when there was a rap on the door. "Yes," he said. "Who is it?"

"Clay, may I see you for a minute?"

He knew the voice. He said nothing as he pulled on khakis, then opened the door. "How are you feeling?" he asked, his voice sincere.

"Do I have to stand in the hall?"

"I am...," no, I am not, he thought, I am not the least bit sorry. "I'm surprised to see you," he continued. "Come in." He reached for a shirt as she entered.

"I didn't show it, I know, but I was very glad to see someone come crashing through that door last night. Then, when I realized it was you...I tried to say something...but I just couldn't, I couldn't say anything. You know, nothing like that has ever happened to me. If I hadn't been to the bathroom earlier, I'd probably have wet my pants...or worse. I was scared, Clay. That Melody, you know, Jed's wife, was so nice and so understanding. She stayed until just a little while ago. Anyway, I was thrilled that you came to my rescue, and I wanted to thank you...I wanted to last night, but she suggested I wait. Clay, I saw a side of you I didn't know existed. That door is still in shambles."

Kile tucked in his shirt. "Two things, Meliss. One, I didn't know it was your room, and the other, you never gave me a chance. You only saw what you wanted to, an unfortunate situation and one you capitalized on to the point..."

"Clay," she interrupted, "I didn't come here to argue over what we once didn't have. You were the one who wouldn't let go. You were the one who kept calling and showing up wherever I happened to be. I almost had to get a restraining order, if you recall."

"You could have let me down with a little more understanding. Oh, forget it—that was then. I admit, I was stupid. It was a case of temporary insanity. I guess everyone is entitled to that once in their life."

"Then we can forget the past?"

"Can you?"

She stepped toward him and put her hands on his waist, as she said, "Yes, you are different now."

"Look," he responded, "I've got some complicated problems right now, and a gratuitous offering of affection is not what I need. Besides, I..."

"Clay, you don't have to explain anything. I merely wanted to say thank you. I've done that, so I'll leave."

As Meliss closed the door, Kile regretted not only what he'd said, but the way he'd said it. I could have been less defensive, he thought. Oh well, it probably wouldn't work any better than it did before, so what's the difference? I'll have breakfast, walk along the canyon trail, and decide what I'm going to do and how it's going to be done. He then remembered the money and the certificates.

He removed both from his bag and stacked them on the floor. Carefully opening the fabric that closed off the bottom of the box springs, he inserted the evidence of his alleged guilt. Using dabs of toothpaste, he secured the thin fabric flap.

Clayton Kile walked for an hour and a half, exhilarated by the view, the grand depth, and colors of the canyon and a very simple fact of something physical. He rested briefly against the bracing of an old stump in the shade of three small junipers. I haven't done anything like this since my Boy Scout days, he thought. How could I have forgotten how great the outdoors is? Have my goals and priorities subverted everything else? Got to get back and call Jim Murray again, or at least talk to one of his partners.

Halfway back to the lodge, the trail dipped below a promontory and skirted an edge of the canyon. There were several large recesses constructed to allow hikers safe passing. It was from one of these that a man suddenly appeared. "Enjoy your hike, Clayton?"

Kile, startled, did not recognize the speed shop owner from Compton. "Who…?"

"It doesn't matter now, does it?" the man said, as he lunged toward Kile with surprising agility and swung a fist to his face. Kile did not see the glove Burt was wearing on his right, nor did he know it was lined with powdered lead. He was able to deflect a direct hit to the chin, but it caught him high on the left cheek, near the ear. As Kile staggered, another blow got him in the stomach. He retched as he sank to his knees. An image of a man in an aloha shirt flashed in his mind. Again the weighted glove struck, and Kile, half-conscious, dropped forward. The last feeling was that of a painful impact to his side. The last sound was a challenging yell followed by someone else's scream of pain. He did not see his adversary stagger and disappear from the trail. Neither did he see the face peering from a cliff high above.

"If only I'd been closer," Señor Vargas muttered, as he stooped to examine the victim. He then wondered if the body, caught some hundred meters below the trail in a jumble of oak, was that of a crossroading dealer or a thief who had known of the money.

Clayton Kile was vaguely aware of being carried in some kind of stretcher. With the acute stab of pain, as one of the bearers stumbled, his nervous system elected to put him under again. His next recollection was the crowd and voices as he was carried through the lobby.

"Can you hear me, Señor Kile?" a voice asked.

Kile opened his eyes and realized he was in his room. It was Captain Rosa who spoke.

"Yes, but I'm not sure I want to. Is there a doctor near here, or a hospital?"

"There is a doctor, a *Norte Americano*, coming over from another hotel. The people here have arranged it. There is a medical facility in Creel, but, as you know, transportation would be difficult. You should not be moved until a doctor sees your condition. Do you understand?"

"Yes, now pour me some of that scotch, please."

"That might not be wise, Señor Kile. At least until after the…"

"How soon will he be here?" Kile said, not waiting for Rosa to finish.

"I can not say."

"Then pour me a damn drink."

Captain Rosa shrugged. "You have great pain. Of that I am sure." He reached for the bottle and a glass. "That is truly a fascinating piece of quartz," he said, as he handed Kile half a tumbler of liquor. "Can you manage or shall I hold it for you?"

"I can handle it, thank you." He swallowed the contents in three gulps and held the glass toward the captain.

"No more, Senior Kile," he said with emphasis. "I now have some questions."

"Yes," Kile said, with a kind of welcome resignation. "I'm sure you do."

"What are you really doing in Mexico, Mr. Kile? You have been in my district for only a short time, and two deaths are directly related to your presence. That does not seem to be a coincidence."

"Two deaths?"

"A man was found below the trail from where Señor Vargas found you. The señor also said there had been fighting. My officers and some locals retrieved the body. It is waiting movement to Creel."

"Look, Captain, I didn't know either one of them. I…"

"According to the woman, Miss Courtland, you knew the *Norte Americano* in La Paz. Is that not true?"

"When did she tell you that?"

"After I asked her to look at the body. She was sitting here with you when I arrived. She'd cleaned up your wounds, and I thought she might be able to help."

With a puzzled frown, Kile reran his recollections of the encounter. As he pictured his attacker, an aloha shirt appeared, and then the face of Burt imposed itself. "It was him, Captain. I didn't recognize him because he wasn't exactly the same man. How did he get here? What did he want? I didn't really know him. He simply intruded."

"I was hoping you'd tell us. Now, the fact that we have a murder…"

"Just a minute, Captain Rosa, I did not kill that man. Sure he, for reasons I…" Kile stopped and thought. Was Burt in some way connected with Heritage? Trevis Thayne and

Dove—was he involved with them?

"What is it, Mr. Kile? You seem confused."

Before Kile could formulate an answer, there was a light tap on the door.

"Yes," the captain said. "What is it?"

"The doctor is here, Captain."

"Send him in, please."

A young man entered.

"Since there is nowhere you can go, Senior Kile, and my officer will be at the door, I will leave you in the hands of...what is your name, Doctor?"

"Ross, Captain, David Ross. But I want you both to know that I just recently finished my internship and am taking a short vacation before settling into residency. I am not giving excuses, just letting you know."

"Do you have difficulty with that, Señor Kile?"

"Not in the least, just do something before the scotch wears off."

"There's one other thing, gentlemen, I'm not licensed to practice in Mexico. I certainly don't want to jeopardize my professional career by getting involved in malpractice problems or ending up incarcerated on some criminal charge."

"Doctor Ross, you have my guarantee, as a career officer, there will be no problems in the latter regard. As to the other matter, I believe Señor Kile will appreciate anything you can do. Besides, you are not doing surgery, you are only examining him to see if it is practical to take him to Creel."

"Any blood in the urine?" Dr. Ross asked after the captain left.

"Not that I...I haven't been...if you'll help me up, we'll find out right now."

"Let's do a quick once-over first. Don't want to compound any probable trauma."

After several minutes of checking and treating the obvious, he said, "I was given the impression you were thrown or pushed into the canyon. I wasn't looking forward to mass injuries, not in the least. Now, deep breath again…again… okay, lean back and relax. Assuming there is nothing internal, no guarantees, mind you, I would say our biggest concern is the probability of cracked or broken ribs. May not even show in an x-ray. Now, let's get you into the bathroom, and then I'll poke through the bag and see what I have for that pain. Doubt if they'll take one of my prescriptions locally, but our priority now is getting you in for pictures of that chest." Kile slept a full hour after David Ross left, the capsule numbing his emerging pain.

chapter
eight

Clayton Kile was just waking when conversation from the corridor filtered into his consciousness. There was a female voice; it seemed in charge. The door opened.

"Oh, I guess I timed this right fine like, you're awake." Melody, the Texan's wife, smiled and set a tray next to the crystal.

"You will have to pardon my slowness," Kile slurred. "The doctor..."

"Now, you just never mind, I brought your dinner."

He slowly adjusted his position as she fussed with the pillow. Her mannerisms, her appearance, gave him the impression she might have been a nurse at some time, or in show business. She seemed quite sure of herself.

"Now there is a problem here," she said, holding the tray.

"Think you could sit at that table by the window?"

Kile wanted to say something pleasant, something endearing. He just nodded, however, and mumbled, "I think so," as he moved from the bed.

"That's a right mean bruise. Here, let me help you."

Impressed by her gentle strength, he eased into the chair and began to eat.

"Not very gallant of me," he apologized, "eating in front of a lady and being almost naked."

"Honey, I was in a chorus line for a couple of years, so think nothing of it."

Kile, as the night before, found it amusing and ironic that his appearance did not make him uncomfortable. He looked at the crystal and wondered.

Pork chop down to the bone, potatoes and gravy gone, he pushed a green vegetable to the side and reached for a light-colored pudding. "How is Meliss feeling?"

"Fit as a bird on an early Texas morning, Clay. She's out doing her thing, said it's best when there's shadows, whatever that means."

"Someone said she did the cleanup and first aid when they brought me in."

"I don't know. She didn't mention it. We were on a ride when all this happened. Jed figured we might as well be doing something instead of sitting like a bug on a dung heap. He sure got impressed, the way those little old men dart up and down that canyon. Said he'd like to have a few of them on the ranch. He's real pleased we came here, with what's happened and all."

"Who found me and brought me in, do you know? The captain said something about Vargas."

"Don't rightly know. Meliss thought it was a bunch from the hotel, some guests that were already here."

"That was delicious, and I thank you."

"Y'all are entirely welcome, glad I could help. Clay, Jed told me not to pester you with woman curiosity, but why on earth was there a fight with that terrible man? Meliss said he was a real bore and that she saw you with him in La Paz."

"I wish I knew, so does the captain. He thinks I might not have been the victim. As for knowing this Burt, that's wrong. He was just there, kept popping up. I didn't even recognize him when he jumped me."

"I'll take the tray now and let you rest. Don't tell Jed I asked anything, okay?"

"You didn't ask a thing, and thanks again."

"You are right welcome, honey." She winked and added, "Now you get some rest, hear?"

Kile considered getting dressed. I'm not shaky, he thought, as he moved about the room. He looked at the canyon, now completely different in the approaching darkness. She called me Clay. I wonder what else Meliss told her? The impact of pain changed his mind about doing anything except looking for the two capsules left by Doctor Ross.

"I should have taken one before I ate," he said to himself.

The voices in Spanish outside indicated he was about to have another visitor.

"Señor Kile," Captain Rosa said as he entered and closed the door, "the man was a private detective from San Diego. Does that mean anything to you?"

Kile shook his head.

"I also am to inform you that we are to hold you for the authorities in San Diego and your federal officers."

"What the hell for?" Kile asked in anger. Yet he felt he knew. He returned to the chair.

"I was not told. But, as you would say in your country, I think you are in deep shit. May I have permission to search your room?"

"You'd do it anyway, wouldn't you?"

"Yes, but I am a gentleman, Señor Kile. We are not as primitive as some *Norte Americanos* seem to think."

As Captain Rosa began his search, Kile, about to make it easier for him, heard Melody's voice again confronting the guard.

"Well I don't care, she hasn't returned and I want to see the captain and Mr. Kile right now. You hear that?" Captain Rosa also heard and opened the door. "What is the problem, Señora?"

"I want you and your men to look for Miss Cortland. It's after dark and she was to be back over an hour ago. I asked the hotel people and they said to see you."

"I do not have any men, Señora, and Mr. Kile is now in custody for additional reasons. The present guard will have to be relieved soon. Have any of the staff looked for her? This sometimes happens. Tourists go walking, they do not take lights, they lose direction, and they become lost. I will talk to the manager."

"Captain," Kile said, "if you remember, this woman was subjected to a very traumatic situation. She was about to be attacked. I suggest you take this more seriously. She is not the type to do something stupid."

"Just how well do you know her, Señor Kile? Perhaps I should see if she is also wanted."

"She doesn't have anything to do…"

"To do with what, Clayton Kile? Please go on."

"We knew each other years ago. It didn't work out. I ran into her in La Paz. There's no connection, I assure you, with this…this Burt thing. By the way what is his real name?"

"Are you evading my question, Señor Kile?"

"No, absolutely not. I didn't even know it was her room. You remember my telling you that, don't you? And I don't have the slightest idea where she now lives."

"His name was Albert Keck," Rosa said, taking a different tack. "He was of questionable character. I am sure the San Diego authorities will check his office and his clients. It also appears that his license was in the process of being revoked. What are you doing, Mr. Kile?"

"I'm getting dressed, I…"

"Clay, you're not going anywhere," Melody interjected.

"She is correct. You are in custody, remember?"

"I was thinking of his injuries, Captain."

"Señor Kile, and Señora...?"

"Melody Surrat, Captain, or if you prefer, Mrs. Jed Surrat."

"Thank you. As I was about to say, even though my country has Napoleonic Law, I do believe in certain rights to persons under my jurisdiction and in my custody, at least rights of consideration. I will check into this matter. Remember, the local ethnic group here, the Tarahumara, are a proud and independent people. If the woman is lost, I will call on their *raramuri*, their runners. However far she could have gone in an hour or two they can cover in a quarter of the time. Señora Surrat, after you."

As they exited, Rosa said something in Spanish and the guard entered. "Señor, I am to continue the search of the room. No problem, please."

"Can you have a scotch, some whiskey, with me?"

"Another time, *gracias*. Please go to the bed with your drink."

"How about just staying by the window? I need to move a little."

"If you want the window, you have to sit," the guard said, with obvious irritation.

Kile was not sure whether the young officer was nervous, didn't like him, or simply doing his job. I could make him a hero, he thought, and show him where the money is. I wonder just how honest and ethical the captain would be? Damn, I could be shot trying to escape. They obviously don't know about the money or this place would be ripped apart. If I was set up for theft or embezzlement, why hasn't something happened? Kile chuckled at his ridiculous thought.

The guard glared. "Why do you laugh? You think I am stupid?" The searching stopped. He waited for an answer.

"No, no, not at all. I was laughing at my own stupidity, the funny way I was thinking. The past few days have not been my usual lifestyle."

"I do not understand."

"My whole life has been office work, dealing with facts and figures, not people. Now, in two or three days I have been subjected to an earthquake, a plane wreck and injuries, confronted with some kind of burglar or potential rapist, attacked on a mountain trail and beat up—possibly an attempted murder—and now I am being held by Mexican police. Isn't that a bit unusual?"

"If what you say is true, *lo siento mucho*. I am very sorry." He stooped to look under the bed.

Kile finished his drink and leaned forward, putting his head in his hands. I might as well tell the captain about the money, he thought, because there is no way under the circumstances that I'm going to get it out of here. In fact, if he keeps poking around he'll find it. Then how will things look?

Voices in the corridor brought the guard to his feet. He brushed off and smoothed his uniform, then opened the door for his captain. Rosa was followed by Doctor Ross. "I found nothing, my captain, but I wonder about the crystal."

"That does not come under the new mineral laws. Did you buy it from vendors, Señor Kile?"

"Yes, but to hell with that. What has been done about Meliss Courtland?"

"You are forgetting that I am in charge here and you are my prisoner! I will ask the questions! Except, of course, for the doctor. Sit down, Kile."

The doctor shrugged and said, "How do you feel? Any improvement? Anything worse?"

Kile looked at Rosa then back to Ross. "I suppose I'm not suffering any severe injuries but I am sure as hell sore. What about the x-rays?"

"That's what I came to see the captain about. I'll also bring your mind to rest about the search party. There is a group of about fifty, with flashlights and torches, checking all the trails in the vicinity of the hotel. That's all that can be done until daylight."

"He is correct," Rosa added. "It is what I would have

explained had you not been impatient. Now, as far as the trip to Creel, I first must ask you, Doctor, can it wait until tomorrow, after the authorities have talked to Señor Kile?"

"Will the track be cleared by then?"

"It is possible."

"Then I see no reason for an aggravating trip tonight."

"Good, I'm glad you see it that way also. I would not want to subject him to such an uncomfortable journey."

Turning to his subordinate, Rosa said, "You will be relieved soon. Return by eight tomorrow morning."

"Let's take another look at you," Ross said. "Just a precaution."

"I will be outside, gentlemen, watching for the relief officer."

As the door closed, Ross quietly asked, "What the hell is going on here, Kile?"

Clayton Kile frowned as he said, "Doctor, you wouldn't believe it if I told you."

"Try me."

Kile repeated what he'd told his guard, but more slowly and deliberately.

Before Ross could respond, even with some doubting declaration, Rosa opened the door. "If you are ready, Doctor, I will return you to your lodge." It sounded more like an order than a question.

"I'll try to get back in the morning. I don't think the slide will be cleared before noon."

"Good-bye, Dr. Ross. Thank you. I will gladly pay any bill."

"Don't even think about it. After all, I'm not licensed to practice here, remember?"

"I will leave instructions," Rosa added, "that you are to be informed immediately of any search results."

As they exited, Vargas arrived, saying, "One of the *raramuri* found some camera parts, Captain. He's waiting on the verandah."

chapter
nine

The rapid sequence of events at Heritage Savings and Loan, culminating in the hold on Clayton Kile, happened as a result of the involved agencies finally coordinating their investigations and sharing information.

The DEA, responding to the leaked information about Kile and his briefcase, followed the matter carefully and diligently. They wanted him, his contact, and the transaction, as a corollary to the investigation of money laundering at Heritage. The field agents were also concerned over the new route for Colombian deliveries forced by losses in the southeast, the usual drop zone.

The questionable practices and apparent poor judgment of the Heritage movers and shakers warranted receivership, but no arrests. The drug money passing through their laundry did.

The abrupt closure caught Trevis Thayne, his son, and Clarence Dove on the premises. Professing regret and innocence to the several state and federal agencies involved, they quickly pointed to the disappearance of Clayton Kile. They assured everyone of cooperation. They did not expect arrests. The coronary suffered by Dove eased the anxiety of the Thaynes.

"It will just be a matter of time, son," Trevis said, as they waited for their attorney. "Keep your wits and be patient. I've planned this carefully, and even though it will be rough at times—I didn't think it would come to an arrest—we will live rather well once it's over. Remember, I covered a lot of bases and I once told you that I was not about to give up my lifestyle. We can not, however, quickly post bail, whatever it amounts to, for the simple reason of not having the money. Do you understand?"

Trevis Jr. nodded. He did not look well.

"As to Clarence," Trevis continued, "we may have a problem, especially if things do not go as planned in Mexico. I should have heard something by now. In any event, Dove may not recover, so why worry?

"Dad, why did you bring him in? You wouldn't have..."

"The name, son, the name. We needed that and his ecclesiastic appearance to further the image of Heritage. I had to take the risk, and it was worth it."

"How much are we telling our attorney?"

"Eventually we'll end up with different lawyers, but for now one will represent. A delaying tactic will be conflict of interest, but we'll let the court, Dove's attorney, or the prosecutor initiate that. Regardless, you know absolutely nothing, this has been a total shock to you. You can't believe this is happening. But you never did trust Clayton Kile. There wasn't anything specific, it was just a gut feeling of distrust. Oh yes, you did see him, on two occasions, with some rather unsavory looking characters. Do you understand? And I want you to firmly fix in your mind, right now, where each incident occurred. Don't worry about specific dates, remain general. Neither was important at the time. Now get back to looking bewildered, we are about to have company."

The limited statement of Clarence Dove, from an intensive care unit, consisted of repetition of one name, Clayton Kile. That cemented him as a prime suspect and gave some degree of credence to information provided by Thayne's attorney.

The civil actions being filed were thrust into limbo as criminal charges regarding money laundering, fraud, embezzlement, and theft made headlines.

chapter
ten

As Captain Rosa examined the camera part, an 80 mm lens with case, he stated to Vargas, "We have no proof this belongs to the woman, do we?"

"Perhaps we should ask Señor Kile or the Texan's wife. One of them may know. If you can not spare the time to follow the runner, I will do so in your behalf, Captain."

"Would there be any value in looking in the dark? One thing I wonder about, Señor Vargas, why is a man of your position—you have cattle, a lumber mill, and mining interests—waiting here for the clearing of the tracks? Any number of your people could have arrived to transport you. You have vehicles and horses."

"In answer to your first question, I will say that if it is

possible the Cortland woman is anywhere near the location of this find a thorough search should be made. I will lead it myself. As to your other concern, I am in no hurry. There is no need to take men from their work. Also, I more or less convinced Señor Kile to buy a large crystal. I agreed with the vendor that it would have all sorts of benefits. Such has not been the case, and I feel a little responsible."

"Are you sure it's not the woman, Señor?"

Vargas ignored the question. "Can you tell me why he is being held?" Vargas was concerned, as he had received nothing from his contact.

"I can not do that because I was not told. The authorities will arrive sometime tomorrow with the proper documents. If you will go with the *raramuri*, I will arrange for some help. They will not be my men. If anything is found of importance, have the hotel manager relay the message to me. I shall return in the morning. I do have other duties."

"I understand, Captain, and I do want to help. The Mother Mountains are my home too, remember?"

"Of course, and I am aware of your concern. But, as in the case of Señor Kile, I feel there are things not being told."

"What is there to tell, *amigo*, when nothing is known? I must go if I am to coordinate the search. *Adios*."

The three-hour search revealed nothing. Vargas had beer with some of the search party, dispatched one of the runners to inquire lower in the canyon, and returned to his room.

Zlatec, the one who presented the camera part, the one asked by Vargas to check with his people, went directly to Callo, the shaman.

"*Kwiri ba*," he said, as he entered the *galiki* some twenty minutes later.

The shaman returned the greeting and motioned for him to be seated. "Did they believe the information we suggested?"

"Yes, Speaker, and they will search that area again in daylight."

"What can you tell about the one who has the crystal?"

"Only that he is kept in his room. There is a guard. His food is not taken by the waiter. A maid does not clean."

"It is sad that Tatla had to die. He should not have been the one to go after the crystal."

"That is true, Speaker. He was the best of the *raramuri*, but he did not think before he did something."

"Yes, he was impulsive. He went to the wrong room, is that not correct?"

"Yes, he went without listening to others. He wanted to be seen in the eyes of the council. In death will he cause mischief?"

"I do not think so. He is in peace now for he chose death and said nothing, but we never know for sure."

"The man who fell to his death when I threw the stone—will his soul cause trouble? It was necessary to do it for he would have killed the other one and taken his possessions."

"No, his spirit can not, for he is not of our people. You did what had to be done. He was not a good man. The one you saved from sure death in the barranca is a good man, I believe, from what I feel, but I am puzzled. Why is he held by the police? Is it because they think he killed the man?"

"What I have found out is that others will come tomorrow, Mexican officials and *Norte Americanos*. They will take him."

"Then something will have to be done tonight. Come, we will talk to the woman. We have seen to her safety and care. Perhaps she can help us."

Thoughts did a merry-go-round in Clayton Kile's mind as he tried to sleep. They can't just come here and take me back, he thought, there's something called extradition. They have to go through all kinds of legal maneuvering, unless I waive the process. So they may simply want to talk to me and that's fine. I can tell them the whole story as I see it, give them the money and stocks, and that's it. It's self-evident. Once that's clear, I'm sure the local authorities will see no reason to hold me on the death of Burt. I wonder just how he fits into this thing, anyway? Has to have something to do with Heritage. Yet, if I have the money, isn't that evidence against me? I'll have to take chances on that. I could tell them that if I was going to abscond with corporate funds I surely wouldn't take such a minimal amount. They could say, though, that I put the rest...this isn't getting me anywhere.

Kile shook his head, sat up, then moved from the bed. He started for the window then, thinking of the cash and certificates, decided to get it ready for handing over.

Kneeling, with one hand on the bed for support, he reached through the slit and groped for the packets. His stomach knotted and panic erupted...It was gone, all of it.

chapter
eleven

Meliss Cortland, entranced by the canyon's command, became careless as she maneuvered for shots of colorful shadings and stark promontories.

Thrilled with the last frames of the roll, she hurriedly reloaded to get a few more shots in the fading light. The finished film slipped from her hand, and as she grabbed for it, the Hasselblad 500C, her pride and joy, tumbled out of sight. "Shit," Meliss muttered as she jockeyed for a position to see how far the camera had gone.

A young Tarahumara girl, fascinated by the slender, black-haired taker of pictures, had watched for over an hour. Except for obvious clumsiness in such simple climbing, she admired the woman. This woman tourist was different. But surely she would fall from such a position. The girl stood to yell a warning. It was to late, Meliss was all ready sliding down a smooth face of the outcrop. As she disappeared, the girl heard a cry of dismay, then terror, echo from the darkening canyon edge, then only silence of night.

Smells confused Meliss's mind as she emerged into a semiconscious state. They were not unpleasant, merely different, unlike anything sensed before. Herbal, she thought, definitely herbal. As her eyelids fluttered, she became aware of the dim, flickering light. It was a small room and there were people.

"Can you hear my words?" a coarse feminine voice said.

As Meliss turned her head toward the sound, she heard intonations, a kind of chant. It did not come from inside the room.

"Can you talk, or do you understand me?" the voice said.

"Yes," Meliss whispered as she nodded. "Am I hurt badly? Are there any broken bones?" She was reluctant to move.

"The bones no, inside we don't know. Be still for now. You didn't fall a great distance, and there is only a little blood. The shaman prepared medicine which was rubbed on your injured parts. Can you take sopa…soup?"

Meliss Courtland took the bowl of broth. She knew she had fallen, that there was a period of unconsciousness, and that she was safe. That she was not the least apprehensive did not bother her. Even though sore, she was reasonably comfortable and felt sure there was no serious injury.

"Good, you have taken it all," the stern-looking woman said, her face warming slightly. "Now you will sleep."

"Can you have someone tell the lodge I'm okay? How far away are we?"

"Who will most worry?"

A sudden fear tore away the ease as she realized there could be a connection between the intruder and where she was. Why are they watching me? she thought. Recollection of the man in her room made her shudder. "I have to be getting back to my room, will someone guide me?"

"Go if you wish," the woman said, "but the souls of many

are out and can do mischievous things. I will not go, and the others are now gone from the outside."

Meliss raised herself from the slightly elevated platform that was her bed. Dizziness and blurring of vision weakened the eagerness to leave. She eased herself back onto the blanket and slept.

Zabata, the elderly shaman, spoke, "This was not the thing to do. The authorities should have been told immediately. Keeping the woman will not help us in any way."

The youngest of the council spoke next, "I have to much respect for your years, old Shaman, but knowledge of your time is not for now. The idea of asking for return of the crystal will only cause greater interest and some will want to know where it came from. We will take it, not ask. Unless the woman is of use. Others know the legend, too, and those not enlightened would make the sacred cave a place for tourists...a place for nothing but dollars."

"Carlo is right," said an older member. "For everyone to know would defeat our purpose. The movement must grow slowly, for such an opportunity has not come since the last revolt of the silver slaves."

"Teporaca must be avenged," said Carlo. "Three hundred years is a long time."

"It is your thinking that may be wrong," Zabata said. "It is not the Spanish here now, or the hated priest, Father De Abec, so what is the point?"

"There is still gold in the barranca," Callo, the new head shaman said. "We all know that and we know that it would take great wealth to remove it from the ground. We also know that none of it would be ours, except for what we would be paid for working. Do any of you doubt the Mexican authorities would quickly find ways to show it was not ours?"

Zabata's face saddened. "No matter what the past, the idea of independence, the thoughts of revolt, are..."

"But the people are ready," interrupted Carlo, "and they

only have to be brought together in the movement. We will ask for independence, then we will fight for it."

The elderly shaman knew there would be no listening to his words. He also knew their ideas and plans would bring only trouble. That the cave, lost for so long, would not be the sacred place it was supposed to be saddened him greatly. What can I do, he thought, go against my people, betray my sacred trust? If only the cave could be protected.

"No harm shall come to the woman," said Callo. "The man, Kyle, will not be hurt either. We will take the crystal if he does not wish to sell for return of his cost. Carlo, return to your job. Talk to him, reason for our movement, but do not disclose anything other than it is sacred. Keep us informed by the *raramuri*. Now go."

After the young man had gone, Callo turned to Zabata. "Remember, Shaman, he is the most educated and his eagerness is refreshing. If the movement only restores the ancient beliefs, I will be happy. Will you personally guide the woman to the hotel when she wakes?"

The old man nodded, then said, "Speaker, Carlo was chosen, above all others, to be schooled. First in Chihuahua and then in Mexico City. Was it for the better? If he wants to be shaman, if he wants to bring back some of the old ways, he must....I do not believe he is sincere....There is something in his mind that is not right. Let us have him take the sacred meal and be tested."

Callo waited a few seconds, then said, "I will not remember this talk. Carlo is a member of the council, the youngest ever. I would not say this if others were around, but hold your tongue, old man, for perhaps you live too much in the past."

Zabata again nodded, this time in defeat, and ducked through the low exit of the younger shaman's *galiki*.

Twenty minutes later and fifteen hundred meters farther up the canyon wall, Zabata entered the *galiki* of the old woman. "*Kwiri ba*," he said. "Where is the woman?"

"*Kwiri ba*. She left with Carlo."

chapter
twelve

The panic that hit Clayton Kile was debilitating. With the money and bonds gone, and no idea how or by whom, there was nothing to substantiate his innocence. How else could he lay out his claim of having been set up? Surely they would know of the money; that would be part of the noose set clearly around his neck. If there were losses, and he was now thoroughly convinced there would be, he was certainly the prime suspect.

Who knew I had the money? he asked himself. Who besides Thayne and Clarence Dove? Was Burt connected? Had there been someone in his La Paz room? If so, why wasn't anything taken? The officer, Montoya, could he have opened the briefcase? Then why wouldn't he have arrested me or at least questioned me?

He did not remember the attendant in the rest rooms at Los Arcos, the one who had used a hand mirror to see, the one who would follow him for a chance at stealing more money than he had ever seen in his life.

Clayton walked to the window. How much time did he have? What time would they arrive? Where would he look if he could get out of the room? His thinking changed as he looked into the night sky. "Damn," he whispered, "it's a long way to the ground." He made a closer examination. But, he thought, the eave of the roof is within reach…if I stand on the window sill, I wonder?

Within minutes he sat quietly on the peak of the hotel wing that ran along the edge of the canyon. Exhilarated by his escape, he did not notice the cold, but as he paused to rest, the necessity of other clothing became evident. He knew he would have to return to his room. He felt an inner glow at the thought of what he was doing and the vast changes in himself. He knew the adrenaline surging in his body made him feel good. He could get back into the room and out again easily.

Dressed appropriately, Kile was ready to leave the room for the second time. The crystal, reflecting in the dim light, caught his attention. Without thinking why, he thrust it into his coat pocket and climbed onto the sill.

Again on the roof, he worked his way to a point near the main entrance where a stand of ponderosa thrust their limbs against the eave. With easy access to the trunk of one of the larger trees, he made his way down. It never occurred to him that he had not climbed a tree in over thirty years.

Pausing to decide his next move, thoughts of Meliss intruded. Had she returned? Was she injured? Did her disappearance have…no, of course not. He switched to more immediate problems but was interrupted near the kitchen by arrival of early morning deliveries. He retreated into the oak foliage to wait for daylight.

The first rays of sun did not awaken him; the voice did.

"*Buenos días, Señor*...good morning. Do not be frightened." It was a reassuring voice, but the accent was hardly Spanish. "My name is Zabata."

His mind fuzzy with sleep, Kile could only say, "What do you want?" and puzzle over the rainbow spot on the old man's face.

"We must talk," Zabata said as he pointed to Kile's jacket. The protruding crystal was transforming the early morning light.

"There are going to be men after me." Kile rubbed his neck.

"The *policía*?"

"Yes, but I am..."

"No time for talking. We must move into the canyon. There I will hide you. Come."

Must be burnout, Kile thought as he got up and, with no questions whatsoever, followed the old man into the canyon.

Zabata's stamina was amazing. When they finally stopped, Kile was exhausted. The rest was for him, not the elderly shaman.

"I must leave you here for a short time. You will be safe. There is someone at the hotel to be seen. I will bring news also. Be patient, we will talk at length when I return." The man moved up the trail, sure-footed and steady-paced, as a much younger person would be.

Kile stepped back into the narrow defile and was hidden from the trail. He wanted to laugh at himself, at the situation, and the unbelievable events occurring. Maybe I'll wake up, he mused, and find out someone slipped me some...what is it called?...peyote?

Zabata stayed near the hotel only long enough to talk to some of the men caring for the grounds. The main entrance verandah was busy with people. The railway was now open, and people appeared anxious to be on their way. There were four men talking to the captain. They were not tourists. Three seemed to be *Norte Americanos*. The other, Zabata felt sure, was an official of Mexico. They did not look at all happy.

Zabata remained in the trees until one of the workers

returned from the service area and gave him the information he wanted. He then took an older, less secure, trail as a shortcut to avoid anyone who might be on the main path.

A series of flute-like whistles alerted Clayton Kile. Then a familiar face said, "It is Zabata."

At his urging, they hurried farther into the canyon. "There is not yet time for talking," he said.

Half an hour later, Zabata suddenly sidestepped into a crevice, Kile followed, and they were on a trail leading to a small ravine. Ending in a cul-de-sac, the trail led to a cabin-like structure protruding from the wall of the barranca.

He was impressed by the apparent greetings of "*Kwiri ba*" and other strange sounding words, but more by the obvious deference and homage paid to his guide.

"We will have some food here," Zabata said, as a woman and her two children reentered the *galiki*. "Their home is small, so we will sit here in the shade. This is called a *dekochi*, it is a cornhouse, a granary." It was a smaller, shedlike building above and to the right of their dwelling.

"Try some of this," the old man said, offering a clay jar. "It is what you would call beer. In Spanish it is *tesquina*, but in my language it is called *suquiki*. It will not be as cold as you may like."

Kile, though not having a particular liking for beer, drank eagerly.

The woman then brought a stew of vegetables, some tortillas, and chunks of pineapple.

"The fruit comes from low in the barranca," Zabata said. "The woman is sorry she does not have meat."

"I don't mind at all," Kile said. "This is delicious. I would like to pay her something."

"No, that would not be done…because of me. You might leave something behind when we go, something where you are sitting."

Kile nodded in understanding.

Zabata looked directly at him. "I do not believe you killed

the man, for I know of someone who said he threw a stone, pushing him into the barranca. He saw you fighting the man after he attacked you. What was it about?"

"First, I have a question. Was this man you know of following me?"

"Yes, but not to harm you."

"Why?"

"For this," Zabata said, tapping the pocket of Kile's jacket.

"For god's sake why?"

"You have had your question, now answer mine."

"I'm not really sure why. How is it you speak English so well? Are you related to the woman here?"

"I was in the Catholic school and later an altar boy. The priest had been for many years a teacher of English. No, the woman is not a relative but is of my people, my flock…but no, that is not quite true, for I am no longer the chief shaman, I forget. As you can tell, my voice is failing, and we have a speaker. I am still on the council and that is why I am doing all this with you. There are many things I have to tell you, but I must know one thing now. Is this crystal of value or importance to you?"

"Is it important to you?"

"It is of very old religious…it is sacred, that is all I can say. Now, please, the man who died. You have not said why there was fighting."

Kile explained as simply as possible the predicament he had been led into. He talked for half an hour, ending by saying, "There are things that are not clear, things I hope to find out. One logical reason for Burt to kill me would be to make sure I didn't get back. Or, if he knew of the money in some way, it could have been simply that. By the way, do you know of the woman, Meliss Courtland, who was missing? Is she back at the hotel?"

"Is the woman a friend?"

"She was.…We were once very close, but that was years ago. We were not traveling together."

"You have feelings for her, so I will be truthful. The woman took a bad fall from the rocks while taking pictures. She was rescued and cared for by my people. I was to guide her to the hotel when she recovered but did not. The woman had been taken away. That is why I was there, near where I found you sleeping. I had to find a man named Carlo. He works at the office of that place but is not there."

"You seem to know a great deal, Zabata. Do you know why the man was in the woman's room? The man who jumped from the window?"

"I can tell you only that he was not there to harm her or steal from her. I can not say more."

"Why did he jump? Was he after this?" Kile patted his pocket.

"He must have known it was wrong. We did not want that done. Enough—we must go quickly before more problems occur. We have a distance to travel. The money, was it taken by the man trying to kill you?"

"It's possible. I don't know. There was hardly time for him go through my room and then get...yes, he could have. God knows where he would have put it. Certainly not in his room. If he did, someone must have found it by now."

"My people at the hotel said there was a strange person, Mexican, who seemed to be looking for someone. He was not a tourist and did not stay there. But come, we must go faster, the spirits tell me there is danger for...for a person."

Instinctively, Kile knew the shaman was referring to Meliss.

chapter
thirteen

When Meliss Cortland awoke the second time, she saw a young man with classic native features.

"How are you feeling, Miss Cortland? I am from the hotel. You may have seen me in the offices. I am Carlo. The name is adopted. I am Tarahumara."

"Am I glad to see you! I was beginning to feel no one cared."

"Can you walk? I'll arrange a litter if not."

"Just a bit shaky," she said as she put her hand against the wall and stood up. "But I do want to get back. Do they—at the hotel, I mean—know I'm all right?"

"Yes, word was passed to your friends. Are you hungry?"

"No, but I would like some water."

"I don't think that would be a good idea. You are not used to our water. I will have the woman bring you something to quench the thirst." He said a few words in his native tongue, then in English added, "Your camera, do you have it?"

"I don't know. It was in a ravine when I last saw it."

"No problem at all. I'll have the girl who found you bring it later. Do you mind traveling in the dark? I don't have a flashlight with me, but that will present no difficulty. I know the trail."

"I'm so happy that you're here, I'd crawl on my hands and knees, and in the dark too." Meliss had to stoop slightly as she took a few paces around the small room. "I'm fine, let's go."

The woman returned and held out a cup. Meliss drank. Shuddering, she said, "That tastes more like medicine."

"It is, in a way. Let's go." Carlo muttered something in the Uto-Aztecan tongue, and the woman left ahead of them.

"Maybe I'm not as fit as I thought," Meliss said, after fifteen minutes on the trail. "I've got to stop...feel dizzy..." She slumped against the bank, eyes glazed, and slid to the ground as Carlo guided her body to prevent injury.

Within seconds, two young men dressed in loincloths and headbands stepped from the darkness. In turn, they touched fingertips with Carlo. One said, "Yes, she is of beauty."

The other grinned, made a sexual gesture, and returned to the thicket at the side of the trail. He returned with poles and a blanket.

"The package?" asked Carlo.

"It is as you ordered, at the unworked mine," said the one who spoke of beauty.

"Good. Finish the litter. I want to be at the cave long before the sun."

"Is the plan going as you want?"

"Yes, even better. We have money—a great deal of it—and some bonds—papers of value. We would have the crystal now except for the *policía* guarding the man who has it. If that stupid man from La Paz had taken it along with the money, there would be no problem. We are watching, and there is always the woman."

"What will be done with her after...when the usefulness is gone?"

"She will always be useful. She is worldly, a professional photographer, adventurous and curious. She will record for the world our movement for independence. She will be thrilled to be a part of what we are going to do. I will allow her to see the sacred ritual of the morning sun, and she will know my power. Does she not look regal? Careful with that, I don't want her injured. Let's go."

"What of Callo, Zabata, and the others?"

"They no longer matter. Their time has passed. I will be shaman and direct a rebirth of the cult."

Once again Meliss awoke to flickering of shadowed light. There were also strange sounds. Her throat dry, she slurred out a question to the seated silhouette she assumed was Carlo. It didn't sound right.

"Ah, you are awake," Carlo said, as he stepped into the light of several candles. "You fainted. I felt you needed more rest so we carried you here." He handed her a cup, saying, "For your throat."

She drank half the contents before realizing it was the same liquid as before. "You son of a bitch, you drugged me...you drugged me and brought me here." Woozy as she was, she managed to lunge forward toward the now illuminated entrance.

"Stop her," Carlo yelled, "before she falls."

Meliss dropped to her knees as the man stepped between her and the entrance.

"You must understand," Carlo said, as he knelt next to her, "we mean you no harm, but you must be patient and listen, for you have a chance to be part of...a vital part of a great and wonderful plan." Carlo appeared highly agitated as he continued, "Now, move there to the side of the cave and you will soon see a sacred and revered thing—an experience that carried the spirit of the Tarahumara until it was lost some three hundred years ago. It was then the priests and the soldiers massacred our people and thrust them into slavery." His hyperactive appearance subsided as he went on. "A piece of the sacred cluster is missing so what you will see is not quite what it should be. It will, however, give you an idea—a picture you will be able to see—of the future of our people. You are to be a part of it. I knew that when you first entered the hotel."

Meliss Courtland slumped to the cotton mats, the potion taking quick effect as a result of her hunger and thirst. She would not see the prismatic dazzle of the morning sun.

"She sleeps," the more talkative bearer said. "She will not see..."

"I know that," Carlo said. "It makes no difference, as she will have many mornings to see it while she is being convinced."

"What if she does not want to be convinced?"

"If necessary, she will eat the bud of the gods. Then she will see, accept, and understand. Watch—now the rays will soon touch the cluster. Then you both will go for the package. Do not be seen on the trail!"

To add to the dilemma of Captain Rosa being on the spot for the escape of Clayton Kile, the Texans, irate at the meager attempts to the search for Meliss, now converged on him and the recently arrived authorities.

"We'll damn well miss the train then," Melody said. "She is an American citizen here to take beautiful pictures of your canyon, paying lots of our dollars into your treasury, and you are not doing a damn thing to find her. You realize she could be lying in some ravine, dying, or being ravaged by someone like that man who came into her room."

"Come on now, little darlin'," Jed said, comforting her. "You just settle down now, hear? We'll get some action, you just wait and see." He turned to the assembled group.

Before he could say anything, the Mexican official began, "We understand your concern for the unfortunate woman and now that it is full light, the search will continue. Is that not correct, Captain?"

Rosa nodded, and the official continued, "You have to understand, however, that we have had an escape by a man who is under investigation for the death of another of your countrymen. We have priorities, and a suspected murderer is on the loose. We..."

"Excuse me," Vargas interrupted, as he stepped into the group and displayed an identification card. "It is vital that I speak with you immediately. Captain Rosa included, of course." They moved toward the edge of the landscaped area away from the main verandah.

"Well I'll be goddamn go to hell," Jed said, as he removed his Stetson. "That guy was with us all the way from Los Mochis. Can you beat that?"

"I am sorry, Captain," Vargas said, "that it had to be this way, but I'm sure you understand. We did not know who he was supposed to contact and who we could trust...but I can go no further than that. I may have said too much in that regard already."

"You stopped at the precise moment, Vargas," said the DEA agent. "These gentlemen are FBI and U. S. Attorney's Office, respectively. They, too, want Kile. Perhaps we could have a discussion, this is a complicated matter. Vargas, was this disclosure...in public as it were, necessary?"

"Yes," Vargas said with impatience, "and I realize full well that I've blown my cover, as you would say. But Kile was attacked on the trail by the man, Keck, and in no way should be under suspicion or investigation for the man's death. There was a third party, whom I have no way of identifying, that struck the decedent with a rock as he was about to kick the victim, Kile, over the edge. I was some distance away and could not have prevented anything, even by yelling. I am also doubting the validity of what the man,

Kile, was supposed to be doing. He simply did not fit the picture. There was never any action or evidence indicating a large sum of money."

"Then why would he escape?" asked Rosa's superior.

"Who knows?" said Vargas. "He did know, I'm sure, that the United States authorities were on the way. He knew too, I am certain, that our law is still Napoleonic. Perhaps he thought he could clear himself in some way or he had the money you referred to hidden somewhere in the area. What are the concerns, incidentally, of these other agencies?"

The DEA man spoke. "Probable embezzlement, theft, and money laundering. That's all we can say at this point. Now, Vargas, if we could see you for a few minutes?

"Of course."

Within an hour the limited information exchange was completed. The Mexican authorities agreed to drop charges concerning Keck's death, but would not give up on the escape from custody. The search for both Meliss Cortland and Kile had resumed and intensified. A request for another search of Kile's room was granted. The Texans, on the adamant stand of Melody, decided to stay until Meliss was found, much to the dismay of Captain Rosa.

At Vargas's insistence, it was emphasized that Kile was to be told he was wanted only for questioning and the escape, and there was to be no shooting. Vargas did not want Kile dead. He was still not sure of things and wanted an unfettered discussion with him. The DEA agent had said nothing more about the drug corridor or the alleged buy.

Just before noon, one of the search party returned and reported something to Captain Rosa. Rosa then walked to the assembled authorities and said casually, "Señores, I think it is again for murder that we want Señor Kile. Another body has been found on the trail of his escape."

chapter
fourteen

Carlo, alone with Meliss, sat quietly and watched the rhythm of her breathing. He was disappointed that she did not look as casually elegant as when she first entered the hotel. He smoothed the contour of her thigh and became more aroused. "I could have you now," he whispered, "but it would not be the way." He removed his hand and walked to the front of the cave. Can't let my feelings get in the way of what has to be done, he thought. She is part of the plan, though, and I know I can make her understand.

Meliss was still sleeping when they returned and handed the package to Carlo. "The time was good, was it not?" one said.

Carlo nodded. "Yes, you did well. Eat and rest while I think of our plan."

"They will find the body and they will come looking," one said. "What will we do?"

"They will not be looking for me."

"But you are not at your job. Won't they wonder about that?"

"Señor Kile is the one they have suspicions about, and they will not be concerned about an office clerk who did not show up. Now sleep." Carlo opened the packet and began counting.

"Zabata," Kile wheezed, "I've got to stop." I'll never let myself get out of shape again, he thought as he dropped to the side of the trail. When his respiration slowed, he asked, "How much farther?"

"You are worried about the woman. Is she important to you?"

"I'm not sure, we were once very close. At least I thought we were."

"It did not end without pain?"

"It was a disaster, for me at least. I couldn't let go, and that made it worse. I was an idiot and made a complete fool of myself. Let's move, I'm okay now."

"You still have strong feelings for her," the shaman said. He had remained standing.

"Yes, I suppose I do. Nothing could ever come of it because there's still resentment in each of us that won't go away. Still, I want to help her. I have to help her."

They moved steadily along the trail. Kile was relieved that Zabata asked no more questions. Half an hour later Zabata suddenly stopped. He put a finger to his lips and quietly said, "It is only a short way from here and voices carry. Do not talk. Also, the trail is narrow and dangerous, so be careful with your steps."

When Meliss awoke from the stuporous sleep, her thinking was fully alert. Physically she was in limbo.

"Are you comfortable?" Carlo said. "May I get you some food?" He seemed almost apologetic.

She stared at him, thinking, you son of a bitch, you kidnapped me, drugged me, and now you're being nice? What do you think I am, an idiot?

"You are thirsty, I know. Here." He offered a gourd.

"You bastard," she slurred. "You are not going to drug me again." She tried to spit at him but there was no saliva. "I'd kick you right in the balls if I could move, you prick!"

Carlo sneered as he said, "I could have had your body while you slept. I could have you right now; you know that, don't you?"

Meliss, fire in her eyes, bile rising in her system, wished she could move.

"You can be part of a glorious rebirth of the Tarahumara spirit. There will be great wealth…"

"Someone comes!" a voice near the entrance said. "There are two figures."

"Go, both of you, stop them. Do not let them near the sacred cavern. Kill them if you have to but make sure their bodies go to the bottom of the barranca."

"It may be some of the council."

"I do not care. Whoever it is—kill them! Go!" Carlo grabbed Meliss by the arms, pulled her upright, and leaned her body over his shoulders. There was little resistance. He hurried to the rear confines of the narrowing fissure.

The barrage of rocks forced Kile and Zabata to retreat across the grotto that separated them from the entrance.

"You're hit," Kile said as they ducked into a small rift. "Give me your sash, I'll tie it around the wound."

Zabata shook his head, then cried out to the assailants in his native tongue. A few seconds later he turned to Kile and said, "Give me the crystal, I must show it to them. I told them who I was and that you came to return it to its rightful place." There was more talk in the Uto-Aztecan language as Zabata walked into view, holding the faceted quartz against his forehead. He then signaled for Kile to follow.

Kile saw the club hurtling toward Zabata and lunged forward, unknowingly evading the stone directed at his own head. He did not deflect the blow in time but caught the crystal as it arched from the shaman's hand. Clutching the icon, he backed toward the chasm, making a throwing gesture as he did. The two men, looking confused, disappeared into the cavern.

Kile knelt and turned the old man over. He was not dead, but the pulse was slow and he was unconscious. Using the sash, he covered both wounds and placed his jacket under the shaman's head.

"Give us the crystal," a commanding voice echoed from the cave, "or you will never find the Cortland woman."

"What makes you think I want her?" Kile said, surprising himself. "I'm here for the treasure, the gold."

"There is no treasure," Carlo said, as he emerged onto a ledge. "What made you think there was?"

"I was told this was the key," he said, holding the crystal higher and shaking it. He was stalling for time, trying to force some kind of strategy, some plan.

"If you destroy it you will die—you must know that—and she will also die. There are three of us, you can not find your way, and more are coming. Do not throw the sacred symbol into the barranca. It is part of our religious heritage." Carlo paraded before the opening as he continued, "There will be a rejuvenation of ancient customs and faith. The Tarahumara will become an independent nation and will prosper and grow. There are untapped riches in the barranca that only we know. We will soon have the capital to promote these riches."

Kile had not seen one of Carlo's men emerge from the cave and work his way along the shadowed ledge. His attention focused on Carlo, he was not aware that the man was creeping up behind him. In a swift dual movement the club came down and a hand grasped the faceted piece of quartz.

There was a simultaneous double feature going on in the

mind of Clayton Kile as he surfaced into consciousness. He saw himself as two distinct persons doing entirely different things. Then he was not sure which one he was, or if he was, in fact, a third person. As his mind became clearer, he knew that the darkness and finding himself securely tied would have, a short time ago, been terrifying. Now, even not knowing how long he'd been out or exactly where he was, he did not panic. Too much had happened. Thoughts of his dual identity in the dream amused him. An analyst would have a ball with that, he thought. I wonder why there's no pain? I know I was struck.

He listened for any sounds that might be clues to his predicament. There was only an echoing drip of water. If I can make my way to that, he assured himself, I won't die of thirst. As he tested the extent of his bindings, the sudden flash of pain told him exactly where he'd been struck. The club had connected with the left side of his head, neck, and shoulder. He groaned as he moved back to his right side.

"Who are you?" the slurred voice of a woman asked.

"Meliss?"

"Clayton? Is it you?" she whispered.

"Quiet," he said. "I think..." He stopped and listened.

There were confusing reverberations of footsteps and voices. "Don't respond," he whispered. "We might learn something."

The two devotees of Carlo entered the grotto and directed their lantern onto Meliss and then Kile. They spoke softly in their native tongue, and one proceeded to tie gags on the victims. He paused long enough to feel the femininity of Meliss' body. The one with the light kicked at him and they left.

Kile, knowing full well it would be difficult without being able to communicate, tried to recall the direction of her voice. He then heard her muffled sob. Making a resounding moan to assure her of his presence, he snaked his body toward the wall he'd seen in the brief light before closing his eyes. From there he knew he could orient himself toward her sounds. Kile found a perverted pleasure in defying the pain as he snaked his way across the rough floor. Resting at the wall, he again signaled to her. She responded with an equally loud groan, and he started in the presumed direction.

Pausing to rest and listen for direction, Kile realized there was blood on his cheek from the head wound. It was soaking through the gag. He could smell it; his tongue confirmed it.

There was a faint smell of perfume as his knees came in contact with her left hip, and he sensed she was in a sitting position. Working his way upward, he could feel the sobs and nuzzled his head against her neck. It was wet with tears.

After resting, Kile began to explore the possibilities of untying Meliss. She was secured to some kind of pillar. Her hands tied behind it. Contorting his body and inching his way around behind, his fingers finally found the knots binding her wrists. Limitation of his movement combined with tightness of the bindings made attempts futile, and Kile leaned his head against the pillar. As he did, a rough projection scraped his face. Seconds later, after repeatedly catching the fabric of his gag on the jagged nodule, his mouth was free, and he worked the dryness with his tongue. "It's going to be okay," he whispered, "but it will take time."

Meliss grunted an acknowledgment.

Twenty minutes later, with periodic assurances given, Kile said, "There, I think we've got it...just a bit more.....ah, that's it. Can you move your arms?"

A mumble of pain came from the woman as her hands moved from behind and raised to tear at the constricting muzzle.

"Oh, Clay, I..." Meliss choked on the dryness as she twisted to face him. "Thank you, you darling man." Her arms reached out and touched his shoulders.

"How about seeing to my..." Kile was stopped as she pulled his face to hers and kissed him repeatedly.

"Hey...hold it, I'd like to get my hands...Meliss, please?"

"I'm sorry, it's just that I've never been so happy to see

someone in my entire life. They drugged me, you know. Here, can you turn just a bit?"

Clay, hands free, quickly removed the rope from his ankles. "Are your feet tied?"

"I'm working on that now."

"What do you know about this cave? I only got a glimpse when they came in."

"Clay, hold me for a minute, please?"

She felt her way toward him, moving on her knees. Kile reached for her, his arms encircling the slender, sobbing body.

Clayton Kile could not believe his intense response. It had never been this way when they slept together years before. Could things have changed this much, he thought, could I have changed? Maybe it would be different, perhaps she could be a little more understanding...maybe that might not be necessary. He tightened his left arm around her waist and stroked her hair with his free hand.

The sudden flash of light was blinding, the echoing voices unnerving. The yells in Spanish and Uto-Aztecan added to the confusion. Neither Meliss nor Kile had heard their approach. As Kile moved the protecting hand from his eyes he could see there were guns. He did not know how many.

chapter
fifteen

Captain Rosa had not liked the arrival of his superior, nor was he comfortable with so many agents from across the border. The disclosure by Vargas had aggravated this minor irritation. So, when a young officer emerged from the government helicopter and was given a highly deferential greeting while in the process of removing his uniform shirt, Rosa was ready to resign.

"Ah, Montoya," the DEA man said, "good to see you again." They shook hands. "You know why you're here, don't you?"

He nodded, smiled, and said, "Of course, my heritage and knowledge of the area. Correct?"

Rosa felt better when he was introduced as the district officer in charge.

"Were we correct," Montoya asked, "in presuming Clayton Kile would make the buy?"

"It is a bit more involved than that," the Mexican inspector injected. "He's now wanted for murder, and we believe he's somewhere in the Barranca Divisadero."

Montoya looked puzzled. "Wasn't that self-defense?"

"This is a subsequent case," Rosa said, "and points directly to Clayton Kile. Especially in view of his escape."

"Does all this have to do with our concern over the Colombian corridor thing?" Montoya asked.

The DEA man answered, "We don't know for sure. One thing is certain. Areas, the more hidden ones, in the bottom of the canyon are being prepared for cultivation."

"Then it is more complicated?" Montoya shrugged and pulled on the woolen jumper. "Who is the murder victim?"

"We believe he is from La Paz, perhaps you can tell us."

Montoya removed his trousers and put on a loincloth. "If he is from there, I may know him. Let's have a look." He added a headband, a sash, and sandals. "*Kwiri ba,*" he said, without expression, and followed the group toward a shed on the edge of a landscaped area.

En route, he was given a briefing on developments in San Diego, both as to the leak, and the alleged theft or embezzlement.

"Where is the money now?"

"We don't know. It is not in the room, so he must have it with him."

"There has been no transfer then?"

"Not as far as we know, not even a suspicious contact."

"Unless, of course," Vargas interrupted, "we consider the Texans. And, it could have been the other victim...what was his name? Keck?"

A guard opened the door, and Captain Rosa motioned for Montoya to enter.

"Yes, I know him," Montoya said, after pulling back the covering. "A small-time crook, served some time, no known activity in the last two years. Worked at Los Arcos, odd jobs and attendant for the washroom."

"What was he doing here?" Vargas asked.

"Is he in any way known or connected in the other matters?" the inspector said.

"In answer to the first, I don't know. As to the second, he lacked the sophistication. When do we start?"

"Which has priority," the DEA agent asked, looking directly at the inspector, "the drug buy, the corridor, or Clayton Kile as a murder suspect?"

"Let's find Kile, he seems to be the key. Montoya, where do you want to start?"

"Drop me near my grandfather's *galiki*. I'll direct you. There's a terrace big enough to land on. No, that won't work, might damage his crops. Just let me down on the cable. I'll take it from there. How about a radio?"

"What is Montoya to all this?" Captain Rosa asked Vargas as the helicopter veered into the canyon. "I believe I deserve some information. After all, it is my district."

"As I indicated before, I am sorry about not being able to confide in you about my position. As to him, I only know that his father's side is Tarahumara, he is fluent in three languages, and has an extensive education. He is often called upon by our own government and others to assist in various things. Just how he knows the barranca and what the situation was between his father and mother, I do not know. He does use his maternal name."

"My superior and the *Norte Americanos* are consulting," Rosa said. "Are you to be with them?"

"Not at present. They will call me if I'm needed."

"Then let us have coffee. I would like to ask one other question."

Vargas nodded, and they walked toward the side entrance of the hotel.

"How is it you are involved?" Rosa asked, once they were seated and served. "It certainly is not the money, for you are well off with your properties, are you not?"

"Some things I can tell you, some things I can not. At least at this time. Again, for this I am sorry. I too am fluent in three languages, and, yes, it is not for the money."

"Why then? Is it for the adventure?"

"Perhaps, but only a little. You see, I am concerned with what can happen in our country. It is difficult enough here. We do not need drug money and a private army coming in to subvert the little progress we are making. If this thing is allowed, they will first become heroes to the people of the barrancas and then they will control them. Too, there will be factions of our own government that, as the *Norte Americanos* say, will want a piece of the action. When this happens...well, I have said enough. I trust you, as I do not believe you have been influenced. We have to be careful, there are always those who can not be trusted."

"Thank you, Señor Vargas. No more is needed to be said. I understand the restrictions on information. Shall we go? No, Señor, allow me. It is a matter of pride."

"I respect you for that, Captain. Thank you."

The two men left the hotel and were greeted by Rosa's superior. "Ah, there you are." He was accompanied by the United States agents. "We will, as a courtesy to our friends, speak English. To better coordinate, I have been given...that is, we have agreed it is time for sharing more of what we know. Also, there are factors other than the ominous and pervading narcotics conspiracy. I have been informed that Señor Clayton Kile is suspected not only of bringing a great deal of money into the country for the purpose of buying drugs; he is part of a financial conspiracy in his own country and is supposed to have taken the money from his criminal partners. These partners, however, deny any involvement and point directly to Kile. The others were arrested anyway; it seems there was money laundering in their financial company, Heritage Savings and Loan. The persons in custody also deny that. It is possible they may be right, this Kile could have been doing it all. I would doubt this, except for his escaping and two murders."

"With all due respect, my inspector," Rosa said. "Señor Vargas has stated it was not Kile who killed the man named Keck."

"Agreed, Captain, but it seems they were involved together in part of the scheme. You see, the man Keck was a private detective, and my friends here have informed me he was hired by someone at Heritage."

"Somehow," Vargas interjected, "this Clayton Kile does not seem to be that kind of man. He appears not at all devious."

"You are not a professional, Vargas," the inspector said. "You are a paid informant for the DEA and you are doing a service for our own government, but you can not presume to judge the criminal mind."

"I am not presuming anything, Señor Inspector, just stating an observation."

"You are also failing to account for the murder of this man from La Paz. There must have been some contact when Kile was there. Perhaps he was to be some kind of courier. Above all, why would Kile run? He did escape custody, did he not, Captain Rosa?" Rosa nodded. "From the amount of money he has in his possession, to say nothing of how much he has in foreign bank accounts,…well, he must be caught and stand for his crimes. You understand, gentlemen," he turned to the others, "his crimes here take precedence."

"We accept that, but we do want him," the AG man said.

"Of course you shall talk to him, you can interrogate for as long as you want. You may even transport him if he is to be a witness of some kind. Under our supervision, of course." The inspector turned to the approaching officer. "What is it?" he said in Spanish.

"A message from Montoya," he answered, also in Spanish, *"el viejo,* the old one, is gone. He has not been seen for some time, perhaps two days. It also seems there are many things going on in Barranca Grande, things separate from this. He wants to look for his grandfather. He feels there are connections. He will radio again at six."

The inspector nodded, then communicated to the others. "Montoya's grandfather has disappeared. He feels it has something to do with Kile. He will investigate further and contact my officers this evening. In the meantime, Captain Rosa, make arrangements for the arrival of fifty soldiers. There will also be another helicopter, from the army. Tomorrow we will find Clayton Kile. Tell the hotel manager we will be staying here, cancel reservations if necessary or send them on to another lodge. The soldiers will bivouac on the grounds while the search is being organized."

"I shall do so at once, Inspector."

chapter
sixteen

Before Meliss and Kile became fully accustomed to the lights, an order was given for them to again be bound. A commanding voice also said, "Gag, and blindfold too, at least while we decide what to do."

"Señor Mosquera, I will do it myself," Carlo said, "and this time they will not become untied."

"No, my men will take care of it. I trust no one, except my own people. You will, Carlo, if things go well, gain my confidence. What brought all this attention? It isn't something we anticipated. We don't like it at all. That's why I'm here, to see how we can keep the authorities out of the barranca."

"It was through no doing of our own. We had no idea this

man Kile would be coming, or that…"

A shattering scream interrupted as Mosquera's men attempted to tie the wrists of Meliss Cortland. She kicked wildly as she cursed and vowed she would not be tied up again. Acoustics of the grotto compounded the irritating shrieks. The sudden confusion gave Kile needed seconds to react. Dormant instinct detonated, and he saw his chance. As the men were tying Meliss, only one weapon still showed, that of their leader. Shoving one of Carlo's men into Mosquera, both pistol and flashlight were knocked from his hands. Of the two struggling with Meliss one had dropped to the ground clutching his groin. The other, his back toward Kile, had just secured a hold on the woman's arms. Kile swung his fist into the neck, grabbed Meliss and, in a stooping motion, seized a revolver from the falling man, then pulled her into the darkness. The echoing of two languages added to the disorder.

"Don't let your men shoot!" yelled Carlo. "Bullets will ricochet. They might hit the cluster. They can't go anywhere."

"He took one of the weapons, you idiot—a .357!" Mosquera yelled back. "So I'm not concerned with some chunk of quartz."

Once things were quiet, Mosquera swung a backhand blow to his man's face and said, "Let someone take your pistol again and I'll kill you. You understand?"

The man nodded and continued rubbing his jaw.

Mosquera, now less agitated, spoke slowly and emphatically, "This is becoming ridiculous. I want them both dead, Carlo—and the old man, too. Do you know this cave well?"

"There are some areas I don't know, but you have to remember the entrance only became known a short time ago. No one has been told to explore thoroughly. There has… well, you know the story. We discussed it."

"Is there another way out?"

"No, of that I am sure. Let me see what the old man knows. He discovered the entrance and may have some knowledge of the cavern's reach." Carlo walked toward the entrance.

• • •

With no light and only a vague recollection of where they'd been previously tied and left, Kile felt his way along the side of the corridor. Meliss, her rage subsiding, breathed heavily. Clutching Kile's belt, she followed. Muted reverberations echoed ominously. There was a period of quiet, after which Carlo's voice rose in anger. They could not hear that it was over the disappearance of Zabata and the crystal.

After ordering silence, Mosquera said, "We'll put a guard on the entrance, they have to come out eventually. Go after the old man and throw him into the canyon. Carlo, I suggest you start carrying a pistol."

"There is a problem," Carlo said. "Just before dawn some of the council and trusted followers may come. What do you suggest?"

"How many?"

"Perhaps a few, maybe many. I can not be sure."

"If this stupid cult thing is going to cause us difficulty, then I suggest we let them come. We'll kill them if necessary."

"I'll put one of my people to watch."

"Yes, mine will go after Kile and the woman." He then whispered something to the man he'd struck.

"If lights are used they will be good targets," Carlo advised.

"That is what I just told the one who lost his pistol. He will go first with the light. Kile will possibly get off one shot. The flash will be seen, and he will be dead. If things are as you say and there is no other way out, we shall soon have a body for them to find and the search will be called off."

"You may lose one of your men."

"That's his problem, his own stupidity."

"They may still look for the Cortland woman."

"Only as a courtesy; they are after the man. Her body, with no wounds, other than from the fall, will be found the day after his. Now, get me some water."

• • •

Not knowing how far they'd gone or exactly where they were, Kile stopped and whispered, "We'll rest. At least until we see lights or hear them coming. Are you all right?"

Meliss stifled a giddy laugh. "Are you kidding?" she asked quietly. "After what's happened to me in the last few days?"

"I didn't mean it that way. Did they hurt you back there?"

"No, but I think I hurt one of them. Hope you know what we're going to do. Do you?"

"Shhh, I think I heard something." A few seconds later he added, "I guess not. No, I don't have a plan. I only knew we had to get out of there. They are going to kill us, do you understand that?"

"Clay...you've changed, you..."

"Not now, we don't have time. The floor of the cave seems to slope down here, so I'm going to check it out. Don't follow me. I'll move a few feet and give you a signal, a 'psst-psst' thing, then you move on down. Okay?"

After moving in this manner for an estimated thirty yards, Kile began to feel a strangeness. He was also puzzled that there was no sign of their being followed. He gave the signal, and Meliss worked her way to him.

"I don't know why," he said, "but I think we're at a dead end. Give me your belt, I'm going to tie it to mine, add my handkerchief, and work my way in an arc. You will be the pivot point."

"I think you're right," she said as she removed her belt. "The sound is different."

The situation was confirmed a few minutes later as Kile said, "It's the end all right, a kind of cul-de-sac, I think. We must have veered off from the main part of the cave. At least the down slope will give us an advantage. Get comfortable, we won't move from here until something happens."

"And what makes you think we won't be here forever?"

"I'm an escapee, remember? No, you wouldn't know

about that. The police, and probably the army...they're bound to be looking for me...and the money."

"What have you done? What money? I have no idea what you're talking about."

"No time to explain now, it's long and involved."

"Clay," she said, moving against him, "I'm scared. Each thing gets worse. I don't want to die."

"You are not going to die." He tightened his arm around her shoulder, nuzzled her neck, and kissed her.

She responded and whispered, "Clay, make love to me, finish what we started before they came with the lights. I know I'm not very appealing, the condition I'm in and..."

He kissed her again, this time intensely. "I'm not exactly lotion and soap, either." His hands moved down the small of her back, pulling their bodies together.

"I don't care, Clay, and I don't need any preliminaries,... mmmm...you don't have to be so gentle."

There was something excitingly primitive raging in Clayton Kile. The absolute darkness, her compulsive eagerness, the changes in himself—all welded into a frantic demand. Half-naked, their bodies merged. There was a sudden reciprocity of thrusts. A rising moan from her throat, and then his hand over her mouth, made them even more aggressive. The eruptive convulsions were over in seconds, and he removed his hand, embracing her securely as the heavy respiration subsided. "I'm sorry...about the...hand," Clay said.

There was only the sound of their breathing, then Meliss said, "I couldn't help it...it was wild...I would have screamed or something. I didn't care."

The moment of repose over, there was an awkward silence before she said, "Clay, you were magnificent. You have changed, wonderfully so." She nuzzled closer.

"Simply the situation. Besides, we don't have time for analysis or a rehash of our previous relationship." He spoke matter-of-factly as he felt for the pistol. "We are going to work our way out of here." Clayton Kile felt it was just that, simply the circumstances. He did not want to resurrect an unpleasant period of his life. "I can't understand why they haven't followed us. We should have heard them by now, unless they're lost."

"Maybe they don't know the cave either. Can we get back to where we veered off?"

"I'm sure we can. It's just a case of following the same wall back. Keep close and, if we see or hear anything, get down quickly and quietly. Let's go."

"Clay, have you ever used a gun?"

"Have you?"

"Only a shotgun, skeet shooting."

"Then what difference does it make? Let's move."

For the first time, a claustrophobic reaction to the total darkness crept in on Clayton Kile. My adrenaline must be down, he thought, as he edged along the wall. The anxiety was short-lived. Echoing footsteps and reflected light triggered his instincts. "Get down," he whispered.

"Clay, I have an idea that may give us an edge. Will you let me try it?"

"What is it?"

"No time, just trust me and watch. I think there's a little niche here, move back, and it will give you some cover. You'll know what to do." She moved ahead, guided by the vague illumination drifting erratically along the walls toward her.

"*Aye Chihuahua!*" a voice said, as the shaft of light flashed across the half-naked body sprawled on the corridor floor. The man with the light pressed himself against the cavern wall. The one with the pistol, an automatic, crouched behind him, saying, "Look for the other one."

Ignoring instruction, the light stayed on the bared chest of Meliss Cortland. "She is dead? I see much blood on her face."

"You fool, we could be dead. Use the light."

"See, there is no one." The beam returned to the body, and he moved closer.

The intense impact of sound reverberating from the first shot was deafening, the second was barely heard. Kile waited, the rolling flashlight casting surrealistic silhouettes, his ears throbbing from the blast.

"Can you hear me?" Kile said, as the light came to rest at the bottom of the incline. "Are you okay?" His voice had a muffled sound.

"This god-awful ringing is killing me," Meliss answered, as she pushed against the body crumpled across her legs. "I think they're both dead. And yes, I'm fine. Now that's stupid, really stupid. A dead man sprawled across me, I'm half-naked and cold, there's blood all over my face, and I say I'm fine."

Kile picked up the light and stared. Grotesque shadows made the scene totally unreal. "Don't talk. All hell will break loose now." He shut off the light, sat down, and leaned back against the wall.

There was no sound except a steady screech inside his head. That he had killed two men did not bother him. The fact that it didn't, did. His brief introspection faded as Meliss moved against him and put her hand on his thigh. "I can't believe this," she whispered. "Are you sure it's not just a horrible nightmare?"

"It's real all right. There's proof." Kile illuminated the bodies, picked up the 9 mm handgun, then cut the light. "Why did he say something about blood on your face?"

"I picked at a couple of scrapes and smeared some across my forehead and left cheek. Thought it might keep them from shooting if they believed I was dead or injured."

"That took courage, doing what you did."

"Maybe it was sheer idiocy. As I was inching my way along, I thought, why don't we just wait and shoot at the light? But then they were coming into view."

"All I could have fired at would have been the light. Aiming at the flash, they would have killed me for sure. Probably both of us. There was only one weapon, but I didn't know that. I wonder what happened to the others? They must have heard—they had to."

"What do we do now, Clay?" She moved against him. She was shivering.

"Listen...hear it?" There was a counterpoint chant, barely audible, filtering through the cave passages.

"I don't hear anything except the ringing in my ears."

"Maybe I don't either. No, there it is again."

chapter
seventeen

When the amplified roar of the shots reached the antechamber near the entrance, Carlo was explaining to Mendez Mosquera why he and his men would have to leave before the arrival of the council and the dedicated followers.

"That solves the immediate problem," Mosquera said. "How much time do we have?"

Carlo moved quickly to the entrance and returned, saying, "There is no time to leave now. You would be seen. Besides, your men are not here."

"You had better come up with an idea, Carlo, or I'll give them blood for their stupid rituals."

"You must hide then until I can work a better plan. That way you can also intercept your men when they come out."

"What about the soldiers?"

"They too are coming into the barranca. They or the helicopter will probably see our people on the trails. They will wonder why."

"If this wipes out our plans for the canyon, Carlo, you will be a dead man."

"I know my people. I will take care of things. Now, quickly go into the left corridor and hide. Wait for your men. They will have to come by you there. You will all have to be very quiet. It is a religious thing, you know, very sacred."

"How long will it take?"

"Perhaps an hour, if the council stays afterwards."

"And what about the soldiers, what if they arrive before then?"

"I will take care of everything, Señor Mosquera, have trust in me."

"This does not appeal to me at all; I'm leaving. I am not going to hide in some hole like a rodent."

"They will stone you. You have violated…"

"I'll take my chances. Which is the best trail? Maybe you can do something right."

"Go to the right as you leave, take any ledge going upwards. There is a chance you may not be seen. What about your men?"

"That's their problem, and yours." Mosquera disappeared into the predawn light.

"Where is he going?" asked Carlo's man as he reentered the cave.

"Did you see anything of Zabata?" Carlo said, ignoring the question.

"No, and I didn't want to go farther. They are coming in great numbers. He may be with them, no?"

"He couldn't have gone far. He is old and hurt, but he has the crystal, that I'm sure of. Look here for it anyway. Now! Both of you! And bring me the package. If you see Mosquera's men, tell them to hide. It is his order."

• • •

When all of the pilgrimage had entered, in silence, the council took their positions and Callo offered a prayer in the name of Teporaca. The chosen few, numbering less than a hundred, waited for the first rays to shoot from the horizon and pierce the entrance. Only the council had been there before and seen such wonders. They said nothing of the missing fragment.

The sudden, multicolored illumination of the cavern walls was more spectacular than any of them had anticipated. Even the council members were astounded by the brilliance.

"It has been returned," Callo whispered to himself, as soft cries of awe became louder and formed into a chant not performed in unison for three hundred years.

Callo stood and called out in his speaker voice. They repeated his words and returned to the chant. This was done again, and his words added to the chorus. Each time, a little more of their creed and beliefs was vocalized and incorporated into the chant.

It was this moving spiritual scene that Kile and Meliss witnessed as they stood in the shadows at the rear of the main grotto. That's why it was so important, Kile thought, as he surveyed the patches of prismatic colors covering walls and ceiling. It was part of a cluster—their icon. *Zabata has to be here, but I don't think anything should disturb what's going on.* He whispered to Meliss; she nodded, and they moved to a sitting position against the wall.

As the prismatic grandeur subsided, so did the Gregorian-like chanting. It was then they were spotted by one of the council. Callo rushed forward. "What are you doing here?" he demanded, not realizing he was speaking in an archaic form of the Uto-Aztecan tongue. "Seize them, they are probably the ones who come for our treasures."

"No!" a faltering but familiar voice called out. "Do not harm them." It was Zabata, calling from an upper ledge near the crystals, and also speaking in the ancient language. He then changed to a generally accepted dialect of Tarahumara, saying, "The man is responsible for the return of the crystal. He should be honored. The woman was brought here by Carlo. She was told lies. Carlo is the one to be seized, for he has been using us and is planning things of great evil."

Carlo and his men made no attempt to rush for the entrance. It was well blocked. "This is not true," Carlo said. There was no confidence in his statement. "I wanted only for our people to have independence and a better life."

"Say nothing more." It was Callo who spoke. "There are government authorities coming into the barranca, and they will decide. Some of you help Zabata. Quickly. Can't you see he is hurt?" He turned to Meliss and Kile and, speaking in passable English, said, "Our sacred place has been violated not only by outsiders, but by a woman. Never, not even in the time of Teporaca, has a woman been allowed here. The council, no, the gods of our ancestors…"

"Callo," Zabata said, interrupting, "you are the shaman and our leader, but I must explain to you our sacred place has not been made unclean. The woman has been wronged by some of our people. This woman was of great aid to him who returned the crystal." Zabata did not relate in what manner. "Explain to those here, in our tongue."

As Callo talked, Kile whispered to Zabata. When the shaman finished, Zabata again spoke. "This man, Kile, Señor Kile, has told me of great bravery shown by the woman when they were met by the men sent to kill them. Do not think of her lightly, she has great courage and has been through ordeals not meant for a woman. Honor her and do not worry about this sacred place being defiled. Did you all not see the sun broken into rainbows this morning?"

Callo again translated to the followers, during which Zabata asked Kile and Meliss, "What can we do for you?"

"Could we please have some water?" Kile said. "We also need rest. Is there a place? They will still be looking for me."

"We will see to both things. There is a *galiki* not far from here where you will be welcome and can sleep." He called to those nearest him, and a gourd appeared.

"Have some of this," he said as they drank. "It is pinole, corn meal. Chew it with some water, it will be nourishing. We should leave soon."

"What about the men I killed?" Kile was again bothered. The coolness of his statement seemed too matter-of-fact.

"After you are resting, I will come back and see that they are taken care of. I will also tell what is being planned by Mosquera and his people. I heard most of what was said. Then, when you have slept, we will see to your problems."

"What about the money and papers I mentioned. Does anyone know?"

"That I will also discuss. Now come, you can eat as we walk."

Arriving at the secluded structure, Clayton Kile and Meliss Cortland graciously and eagerly accepted the austere accommodations and fell into deep sleep.

None of the three was aware that their arrival had been watched by Mendez Mosquera, whose escape route changed when he saw the magnitude of the search. He, too, would have to avoid the soldiers until his contact could be located and arrangements made for his escape from the area. He knew he was persona non grata in Mexico. He was sure the search was for Kile, not him. But how had he escaped from the cave? He would use Kile as a diversion for his own retreat. He would wait.

It was dark when the wrinkled hand touched Kile's shoulder. "Do not say anything," a voice said. It was Zabata. "They are going to shoot you. You seem to have left a trail of bodies in addition to whatever else you are wanted for. At least that is the word. Come, they are not after the woman and will not harm her."

Kile was aware that he had instinctively reached for the revolver. It wasn't there. It was held by Zabata, who now handed it back. "I did not want to be shot," he said.

Kile was also aware of a slight pain in the small of his back where he had secured the 9 mm pistol taken from the dead man. I still could have killed you, old man, he thought. The outline of Meliss was barely visible as he prepared to leave the stone and thatch *galiki*. For the first time he thought of the irony in how she must look, she of the casual, fashion-plate set. He left the flashlight beside her and followed Zabata. "I won't need it," he said. "She might."

They walked in silence for half an hour, Kile carefully following the footsteps of the old shaman. The vague camber of the moon only hinted at his silhouette as he slowed, moved from the trail, and stopped. "We are being followed."

"How do you know? I heard nothing. I saw no lights."

"I know the barranca. He is a long way off. We can talk while you rest."

Kile was amused that he, younger by many years, was the one needing rest. "You are an amazing man, Zabata, and, I believe, the only friend I have in this vast canyon of the Sierra Madre." He accepted the gourd of water but drank little.

"I do not know much about you," Zabata said, "but my feeling is that you are not the killer they say. Yet you have secrets. Is this not true?"

"I have killed two men, you know that." Kile explained what little he knew about his predicament. He ended his brief dialogue by saying, "Did you find out anything about the money?"

"The package will be at my *galiki*. One of Carlo's misguided followers had hidden it. You see, it was Carlo who killed the man from La Paz, who must have taken it from your room."

"What will become of Carlo? Will he be given to the police?"

"He will be tried by his own betrayed people, we the Tarahumara. When he is found. He escaped. Some still trusted him."

"I need him, damn it, to help prove my innocence."

"That is not the main concern right now. We have to hide you until I talk to my grandson. He has some authority, you see."

"Who is he?"

"He is an officer from La Paz. His name is Montoya. But that is not his real or complete name, only the easy one to go by."

"Is he in his early thirties and good-looking?"

"Yes, why do you ask?"

"I think I know him. We had some conversation after the plane cracked up at La Paz. You know, the earthquake thing."

"He is in the machine flying the barranca now. He looks for me."

"I don't understand. Why would he be here? How do you know he's here?"

"No time now, we must walk again. Keep close, for we shall leave the trail and lose the follower. You will be safe soon and can rest."

Cresting a high point, Zabata paused. A crack of pistol fire resounded, and he fell backward against Kile. Going down with the shaman, he felt for the carotid artery. There was no pulse; the old man was dead. Kile crawled into the brush and waited.

chapter
eighteen

It was during that strange illumination, just before dawn, that Kile felt sure there were two of them. Concentrating on the silence and focusing intensely on each sound, time had not lagged. I've got to find cover, he thought, before there's any more light. They won't come in together, that I'm sure of. He looked toward the shoulder of a ridge where it joined the side of the main canyon. He squinted, centering on the shadowed boulders in the wash.

"That's it," he whispered. "Practical cover and a clear view of where I left Zabata." He then thought, can I get there without being heard or spotted? Adjusting the automatic in his belt, he breathed deeply and started crawling, a few feet at a time, toward his goal. Not knowing when one of them might appear, the revolver was kept ready in his right hand.

Having progressed about ten meters, he paused and listened. The rock his foot rested against gave way and rolled. Kile depressed his body into the talus and waited for the sound of shots. He heard the impact as the rock stopped hard against some larger object. There was still no shot. He waited. There was a faint sound of something mechanical, then it faded. He meticulously picked his way. He had to reach the protection of those boulders.

Watching the skyline for any movement, in addition to pauses for sound, he reached the jumbled deposit in the wash. A ricochet sang out as it powdered rock a foot to his left. "Señor Kile, we do not want to kill you," the voice called out. "That was to get your attention."

He was sure it was Carlo's voice.

"Zabata would have killed you—that's why he was shot. Can you hear me?"

Kile did not respond.

"I know you are all right. Say something."

A different voice, from the opposite direction, yelled, "We are all fugitives, *amigo*. Let's pool our escape plans." That has to be Mosquera, Kile thought. I wonder which of those bastards shot Zabata. He remained silent, checking the four remaining bullets in his revolver.

"I have a rendezvous point and horses waiting," Mosquera called, slightly louder than before. "You can come with us."

Kile clenched his jaw as he pinpointed Mosquera's position. He was sure Carlo was somewhere to the right. There was relief that neither had worked his way above him. The sound he'd heard before resurfaced. He was sure it was a helicopter and felt positive that his negotiators would make some kind of move before it grew lighter, permitting the chopper to make additional sweeps of the barranca.

"The Cortland woman—she has been killed, Señor Kile. What are you going to do about that?" It was the taunting voice of Carlo, who had moved closer.

"I don't believe you," Kile blurted out, regretting that he may have given them confirmation of his position.

"We have to move up the slope now, *amigo*, but we can't trust you, so why don't you throw out your pistol and we'll let it go at that."

Mosquera's suggestion gave Kile an idea, but he would wait until the chopper made them more anxious. He chuckled cynically at his thought of the helicopter being on his side. He was the one it would be looking for.

He heard them talking to each other but couldn't make out what was said. Initiating his plan, he called out, "How did you track us in the dark?"

"It was easy," Carlo said. "Do you not know I was raised in the Barranca Divisadero? And Señor Mendez Mosquera comes from the mountains of Colombia, above Medellin. Besides, you make a lot of noise."

"You don't carry a pistol, Carlo," Kile said. "Why should I worry about you?"

Carlo laughed, fired two shots, and said, "It is only a small one, an extra from Mendez, but it will kill."

"Your last chance, amigo," Mosquera called. "We can wait no longer. Throw out the weapon or we will come in from two sides. You won't be able to kill us both."

"Okay, okay," Kile answered. "You win. But I won't come out. I don't trust you either." He removed the .357 rounds and hurled the pistol into an open spot between his position and that of Carlo. He could hear the whir of blades from the other side of the canyon.

Carlo emerged from a crevice and moved toward the grassy opening. "Now, Señor Clayton Kile, I am going to kill you."

"That is exactly what we are going to do," Mendez added. "You are the only one left that could convince them about our plans. So, you have to die. Also, my friend, you killed two of my men. That can not go unavenged. Not that they were valuable—it is a matter of principle." He too climbed into view as Kile peeked from the small grotto.

"Señor Kile, are you a man or do we..." Carlo did not finish the question. A 9 mm slug from the automatic tore into his chest.

"Shit," Kile said, as he ducked back from Mosquera's four quick shots, frantically working at his jammed weapon. The helicopter tilted from canyon center, altered its muted rotor pitch, and raced toward the sound of gunfire. Someone must have radioed from the ground search, Kile thought.

"Come out with your hands up and no weapons," the amplified voice from the chopper said. It was repeated in Spanish, then Tarahumara. A rapid staccato of automatic rifle fire punctuated the order.

For the first time since...since when, he thought...there was the contraction of fear. If he appeared, who would fire at him first? Mosquera or the chopper?

The airborne loudspeaker again sounded, "Señor Kile, the army will kill you on sight. Become my prisoner, and I'll try to prevent that."

It was a familiar voice, but Kile could not place it.

"This is Officer Montoya, Señor Kile. You have to trust me."

Kile then heard the roll and crash of rocks coming from above and to his right. There was a second burst of fire from the air. Trying to remain hidden from the chopper, Kile moved to where he could see part of the canyon wall. It was Mosquera, ferreting his way along a thirty-degree fault that had caused the slide. Kile emerged from his protection, hands raised, and immediately sensed his mistake. They would be focusing their attention on him and not see Mosquera. Yet if he moved suddenly, they would shoot.

"Move to the open area, and move slowly."

Kile tried to point as the blades created a minor duststorm. "Goddamn it!" he yelled. "Mosquera is getting away...up the goddamn mountain! Can't you see?" He knew they wouldn't hear him. He turned his face to where he had last seen him.

Mosquera had disappeared.

Still lying flat, as he had been ordered, he could hear the soft slap of sandals approaching. The sound of the chopper indicated it was regaining altitude.

"I ought to kill you right now," the voice of Montoya said. "Turn over."

"You are letting him get away," Kile said as he turned and raised slightly. "He's the one who killed Zabata, your grandfather. It was Zabata who was helping me."

"What are you talking about?"

"Mosquera, Mendez Mosquera. He and Carlo were following us. Carlo is dead, over there."

"Where is my grandfather?"

Kile pointed, then continued, "Please, tell the pilot to search the ridge. Mosquera is part of the drug thing."

After contacting the chopper and handcuffing his prisoner, Montoya walked up the incline to where the old shaman lay dead.

When he returned with the body he said, "If I did not have professional integrity I would shoot you without so much as a blink. They should have let me arrest you in La Paz and none of this would have happened."

"I didn't kill your grandfather. Either Carlo or Mosquera did. Don't you see, damn it, they were following us. Zabata was the only friend I had in this whole goddamned canyon, the only one who believed me."

"He was old and gullible. He was trusting. Did he know you escaped? Did he know you were wanted for two murders? If Carlo is also dead, the count is now six. And you want me to believe your reference to some phantom killer? Lay back and put your legs out straight." Montoya removed plastic ties from his belt and secured Kile's ankles. "And that is to say nothing about your problems on the other side of the border, for which you will probably never stand trial."

"They said they killed Meliss Courtland. Did they?"

"The missing photographer? Why would they have done that, Señor Kile?"

"Because they—I mean Carlo—kidnapped her, and she, like your grandfather and I, knew about the drug corridor plan. Montoya, do you have any idea what we have been through the past few days?"

"We do not have the same constitutional protections here in Mexico, so I suggest you save your explanations. It might alleviate your trying to remember what you've said."

"For god's sake, Montoya, you can't be that dense." He did not answer. Instead, he turned toward where he had carried the body of Zabata.

"You must have known something was going on!" Kile yelled. "Otherwise why didn't they let you arrest me? Why are you here from La Paz? This isn't your jurisdiction. Or is it?"

The officer continued ignoring his questions as he gently moved the old man's arms and folded them across his chest. Using the sash, he covered Zabata's face and quietly spoke in the Uto-Aztecan tongue until interrupted by a call from the pilot. It was in Spanish.

"There is no sign anywhere in the area of your alleged phantom. I'm going to move you so he can land."

"There should be some horses and one or two men. He said he had contacts waiting."

"On your feet, Señor Kile, and move slowly," Montoya said after cutting the ankle bindings. "We are going for a ride."

Once in the aircraft, his ankles were again secured and his wrists were shackled by chain to a metal plate bolted in the floor. Both his captor and the pilot put on earphones, ending any communication. Were it not for his being secured to the floor, Kile would have been concerned about the officers reference to "going for a ride." Yet, he thought, they could still dump me. The idea that he could spend the rest of his life in a Mexican prison or be executed by a firing squad seemed totally unreal. Exhausted, hungry, and thirsty, he no longer cared. The whole situation was insane. Clayton Kile leaned his head back and shut everything off.

The sudden tilting of the helicopter—he thought he was in the Twin Otter landing at La Paz—brought him to drowsy consciousness, and he realized they were about to land on the grounds of the lodge.

Looks like a lynching mob, he thought, as he saw a crowd assembled at the apparent landing site.

He cared little about the conversations in Spanish as he was moved from the chopper. He recognized Captain Rosa who—oddly enough—smiled.

Then a voice said in English, "For an accountant, you sure get your ass involved in a lot of problems. What is it, some kind of rebel complex?"

"Who the hell are you?" Kile ask, staring at one of the two men in suits. That they were not local was obvious. There were orders in Spanish, and Kile was immediately led off, halting any further conversation.

They entered through service doors and continued to a storage room that seemed to be doubling as some kind of office and command post. One desk, two tables, a blackboard, maps, and charts, and a few chairs made up the decor. One of his guards pointed to a chair and motioned for him to sit. As he did, Captain Rosa and three men in civilian clothes entered and took places at the desk and tables.

"Clayton Kile," said a Mexican with graying hair, who seemed to be in charge, "you are in a great deal of difficulty. To exactly what extent we are not yet sure. There has been an unprecedented number of murders since you arrived in the Sierra Madre." He turned to Montoya and asked something in Spanish.

"With what Officer Montoya has just said, and other information from where the Cortland woman was found, there are now seven murder victims."

"What about Meliss Courtland, is she all right?"

"She is being looked after by the doctor from the other hotel, the one who thought he was on holiday."

"Is she injured? She's been through one hell of…"

"Señor Kile, we will ask the questions. But, to ease your mind, I will tell you it is only exhaustion and exposure. We will be questioning her later."

Kile was much too tired, himself, to protest or say anything more. He was resigned to the impending interrogation.

It had gone on for an hour when a man, the one who talked to Kile at the landing site, entered and whispered something to Montoya. The questioning was adjourned.

"You are hungry, no?" Captain Rosa asked. Only he and two guards remained with Kile.

"Damned thirsty too, Captain. Thank you for asking."

Rosa gave an order to one of his men and then said to Kile, "The commandant inspector is a fair man, and I don't think he believes you killed all those people, but there is much more to this than I have been privileged to know about. You did escape from my men and that makes me look bad. How many did you kill?"

"Captain, just as I told your commander, I did not push the private detective off the cliff. I did not stick a knife in the man found near here, the one from La Paz. Nor did I shoot Zabata, Montoya's grandfather. I admit the self-defense killing of Mosquera's men and Carlo, and I would have got Mosquera if the goddamn gun hadn't jammed."

When the guard arrived with a cheese sandwich and a cola, Rosa said, "Ah, here is your food. It is not much, Señor, but you are a prisoner. Who is this Mosquera?"

"I told your boss, Captain, I'm not sure, except that he has some connection with Colombia drugs and is trying to set up something around here. I think a drug corridor was mentioned. Does that make sense?" Kile continued eating.

"There are things I do not know and things I can not discuss. I hear people coming; your rest period is over."

The commandant inspector strode into the room, accompanied by Montoya and one of the Americans. He whispered something to Captain Rosa, waited for an answer, and left.

"It seems I must find a secure place to keep you until tomorrow," Rosa said. "This may require a trip to Creel." He took Kile's arm and directed him from the chair.

"We may get you yet, Clayton," the American said, as he looked at Montoya and winked.

Montoya did not return any indication of an understanding or an inside joke. He looked impassively at Kile and said, "It may be that the most recent killing can not be attributed to you unless you had access to a helicopter. It also appears that some of your story of what happened up there this morning may have a ring of truth. Why would you go to Creel, Captain? The risk of escape en route and access to transportation should be considered, should it not?"

"Where the hell would I go?" Kile said.

"It is only if I can not find a secure place here. You see, Montoya, he has escaped once."

"I know that. It also took much longer for me to find...Damn, that's it. He had to have local help."

"Of course I did, that's what I tried to tell the inspector. And you too, Montoya. It was your grandfather. He was my guide and my protector. How else could I have found my way around the barranca?"

"Are you sure it was not Carlo?"

"No, absolutely not. He was busy kidnapping Meliss Courtland."

"What happened to the money, Señor Kile?" Montoya said, changing the subject.

"And the negotiable bonds?" asked the United States agent.

"All I know is that Carlo and his men had it at some time. Just where it is now I have absolutely no idea."

"Maybe it was delivered to this Mosquera?"

"You've got to be joking, or out of your mind, Montoya."

"Let's go, Kile," the captain said, motioning to his officers. "We have to find your place of incarceration."

"We get you next," the North American said.

"Why did you make that sign with your finger, Señor?" Rosa asked, as they entered the hallway.

"Because I don't like the son of a bitch," Kile said. "I don't like his stupid asshole grin. Who is he anyway?"

"He is from your Drug Enforcement Agency. The other *Norte Americano* is from a different agency. I believe it is some kind of federal banking, perhaps the treasury of your country. There was also one of your FBI agents here."

After Kile and his guards left with Captain Rosa, Montoya turned to the DEA man and said, "I can't tell you why, but I'd like very much to believe him."

"I wish you did, along with the rest of your people. We'd love to get him on home soil and nail his ass to the wall with the rest of his money laundering buddies. My traveling companion will get him on the fraud, theft, and embezzlement bit. That goddamned Heritage Savings and Loan literally robbed millions from trusting investors—most of them living on fixed incomes."

Montoya shrugged and said, "Sometimes I think your law is more Napoleonic than ours."

"You know damn well what I mean."

"Of course I do. Come, let's go have a drink."

As they left the main building and started across the grounds, a small wiry man, dressed in the traditional loincloth, sash, and headband, stepped from the grove of evergreens. "*Kwiri ba*, Tlaxcala," he said as he reached to touch fingers with Montoya, the traditional handshake.

chapter
nineteen

Clayton Kile, in stoic resignation, had slept surprisingly well in his cell at Creel and was not at all angry when awakened shortly after dawn.

"Señor, we leave early. The helicopter can not transport us this morning; she is hauling bodies. Your hands, please."

This is one I haven't seen, Kile thought, as he extended his arms and watched the placement of cuffs.

"We will go by rail, one of the small repair cars. Now sit, please." He attached the leg irons. A late-model minibus delivered them to the rail station where another officer joined them.

"You will have to wait for your coffee," the one in charge said, as the gasoline engine was cranked into an operational status. "No trouble, please. We have been given orders to shoot if you try to escape."

"As I asked them yesterday, where would I go? And I do not intend on being shot, so let's enjoy the ride. Okay?"

The officers nodded impassively, signaled the man at the lever, and the open car moved southwest from Creel.

It was not the sudden appearance that startled Montoya, it was the fact that he'd been addressed by his childhood name. Tlaxcala was the name given to him by his grandfather during those periods when he had been allowed to visit the Copper Canyon. "It is a name taken from the great advisor to the father of Teporaca," Zabata had told him. "It will fit you well. Honor this name."

Montoya had excused himself from the American and walked with the greeter, using the Uto derivative in their conversation. "How is it you came to me?"

"The follower and successor of your grandfather said to come. The shaman Callo slept with bones of the ancestors last night and communicated with Zabata. You are not to let harm come to the man who was being chased, the one now in jail. He did not do all the things they say. He and the woman were to be killed. He only defended and protected. That is why our people were burying those two when found by the soldiers. They did not belong here. They came with the man who was planning to enslave us as was done three hundred and fifty years ago. Carlo was a traitor to our people. He was joining this man from South America. They were planning things of great evil."

"Are there some of our people that will come and talk to the Mexican authorities?"

"I was not given that to say."

"Then I must talk to Callo. Nothing can be done for the *Norte Americano* without help from those who saw and heard things. What else do you know?"

"That certain things can not be discussed, sacred things of

ancestral heritage. Do not ask where all things happened. If the Mexican speaker asks too much we will stop, we will not remember. Is it understood?"

"It is understood. Do you know of the young Tarahumara who was killed near where the woman was found?"

"Yes, he was a follower of Carlo. He was going to kill the woman. He was sent to do that. He was in the *galiki* where she slept. He was killed there and taken away."

"Who did this?"

"That is not known. Perhaps it was the soul of someone sleeping."

"How soon will Callo, the shaman, see me?"

"I will come tomorrow at first sun and give you his message."

"I will be here and wait for his word." For the first time in his professional career, Luis Tlaxcala Montoya felt conflicts. He was also bothered by the fact that he had seen his grandfather only once in three years and now the old man was dead.

His guilt was somewhat cleansed the following morning when he showed special deference to the shaman. Callo himself came at the appointed time, accompanied only by the messenger.

Apologizing for his uniform, the dialogue began. It lasted an hour. Accepting that what was necessary had been said, they shook hands in the Tarahumara manner and agreed to meet again that evening. As Montoya watched Callo and the messenger disappear into the canyon, he felt a sudden urge to go with them. The impulse was terminated by the sound of an arriving vehicle.

Montoya, once again the astute officer, walked briskly toward the small bus stopped at the main entrance. Confirming that it was the arrival of Clayton Kile, he moved on up the steps and entered the lodge.

Arriving a few minutes later, Captain Rosa, obviously upset by his prisoner being delivered to the front door, ordered that Kile be immediately transported to the service area. "We can not be causing the guests uneasiness," he said, as he also entered the building.

It was midmorning before Kile was led to the interrogation room. It was there that he saw Meliss. She was signing papers. Kile was not sure what he felt other than relief that she looked fine. Then, as she turned and smiled at the inspector, he recalled how different she'd appeared when he last saw her. It would not be the same now, he was sure.

Meliss shuffled the papers into order, handed them to the inspector, and looked up. "Clay," she cried as she lunged toward him. She was stopped by one of the guards. "My god, what have they done to you? You look terrible."

"I suppose I could use a shave and shower," Kile said, managing a faint smile. He watched her expression change into anger as she saw the leg irons and the cuffs.

"There's absolutely no reason for this," she said, as tears formed and started down her cheeks.

Is it because of me, Kile asked himself, or just compassion for another human being? Damn, she looks good. Will there be a latent reservation, or has all this somehow changed her?

His thoughts halted as the inspector said, "Señor Kile, our apologies. Captain Rosa, have your men remove the restraints. You are still in our custody, Mr. Kile, pending extradition formalities from San Diego. The two *Norte Americano* officers are checking on that now. Now, Miss Cortland, there is one other matter. A rather unpleasant thing, but it must be done. Please come with me. We will arrange for a visit with Señor Kile later." He ushered her out as Kile's manacles were being removed.

"I don't know what happened, Montoya," Kile said, rubbing his wrists, "but I'm glad it did. I was beginning to worry." It was then he realized Vargas was also there. "Nice to see you again. Did you miss all the fun?"

"He had much to do with unraveling all this," Montoya

said. "Vargas was with the search party that found Miss Cortland. But we can go into that later. I'm sure you want to clean up. With the captain's permission, of course."

There no longer appeared to be any enmity regarding Montoya's intrusion, and Rosa said, "I believe there is a room available, Señor Kile. The one you escaped from. Come with me."

After seeing him to his room, Rosa admonished him at some length about the futility of escape, that he was on his honor, and that if he wanted anything it would be put on his bill along with the room. Then, just as he was leaving, he said, "We will have an officer outside the door. A formality, you understand. One other thing, Señor, not that it matters, I did not think you were a person who could have done all they said. Of the things in your own country, I don't know."

"Thank you, Captain, I understand, and I appreciate your thoughts. I have been through too much to try anything stupid."

The room was just as he'd left it, except his toilet things had been placed in the leather case. For reasons he could not explain, he got on his hands and knees and looked under the bed. He felt for the torn opening and found that it had either been sewed up or the springs replaced.

Laughing at himself, he showered, shaved, and crawled onto the bed. He was asleep in seconds.

When Kile awoke it was dark outside. He was more hungry than he could ever remember being. The stiffness from having lain in one position was difficult to work out. A hot shower might do it, he thought.

There was a light rap on the door, and a voice said, "Señor Kile, you are awake?"

"Yes, I was about to hop in the shower. Why?"

"There are officers who want to know when you are awake. I shall have them called."

"I'm not going anywhere. What time is it?"

"*Ocho y media*...eight-thirty."

"Could you ask someone from the dining room to come? I want a lot of food."

"*Por*...of course, *Señor*."

He was still in the shower when the waiter arrived and yelled his order from the bathroom. With most of the discomfort gone, he dried off and checked the still-unpacked suitcase for clean clothes. Things were jumbled around, but his spare casuals were there; nothing had been taken. As he dressed, he regretted not having ordered liquor. "Damn," he muttered, "there was a...ah, there it is." He picked up the bottle and took two large gulps. Then, amused at his crudity, he did the same thing again. A heavy knock precluded a third try. "Come in," he said, coughing slightly.

It was the two Americans, Vargas, and Montoya. "I guess we aren't going to have your ass after all, Kile. At least not in the way we figured." It was the DEA man who spoke first.

"That doesn't mean we don't want you," said the other one. "We can hardly subpoena you, but we want your cooperation. There's another matter of priority though."

"We want Mosquera," Montoya said. "We want him very badly. You are the only one that can identify him. That is only one of his names, I might add. He carries a number of them, I'm sure."

"If we can't nail him on drugs," Vargas added, "there's murder and a few other charges, including illegal entry. One way or another we will have him."

"We will," said Montoya, "if he's still in the country, and we believe he is."

"My intuition tells me you are leading up to something that obviously involves me. Excuse me, that must be my dinner. Come in," Kile said, opening the door.

The waiter, nervous in the presence of the officers, set down the tray and left as soon as Kile signed the check.

"Now, gentlemen, if you don't mind, I'll have my dinner."

"Go right ahead," the DEA man said. "We've eaten."

Clayton Kile wolfed down several squares of steak, then said, "What happened in San Diego? Heritage, Thayne, Dove, and the rest—what the hell was going on?"

It was explained as he ate, alternately by the two Americans with an occasional comment by Montoya and Vargas. First, they said, he'd been set up as a pigeon, that he'd been getting too close to the bilking of depositors and the laundering of drug money. It was pointed out that they put him in a backup frame in case the first didn't work. As the DEA man said, "They loaded you with money and leaked to the administration that you were headed into Mexico for some kind of drug payoff or buy. We alerted the field to keep an eye on you. That was their first mistake, because we wanted your contacts, not just you and the money."

Kile cleared his throat. "That's why Montoya didn't seem too concerned about my presence in Baja. Right?" They nodded, and Kile went on, "You see, I didn't know there was that much, nor did I have any idea about the bonds until I checked it out at Los Arcos. They told me my trip was to set things up for a large and complex real estate deal in Cabo San Lucas, after clearing and negotiating things with someone in La Paz. There was an appointment with a Mr. Xavier Kuntz. Neither of which, most likely, existed."

"That leads to their backup plan," the other American added. "If you weren't nailed on the drug thing they were ready to file charges of embezzlement or theft. You see, we were getting ready to close in and they knew it. What they were ready to do was lay it all on you. You'd be picked up, goods in hand, they'd deny any business trip, and bingo, you're it."

"Then why did Keck—I believe that was his name—try to kill me? How exactly was he involved?"

"Of that we are not quite sure. Dove was vague on that. In case it wasn't mentioned, Dove had a cardiac arrest, was brought out of it, and I guess it scared the shit out of him, because he couldn't wait to confess and implicate the Thaynes.

Seems he'd been set up too, but at that point he didn't care if he talked. Good for the soul and all that. Anyway, as near as he could guess, Keck was hired to keep an eye on you and alert them to any problems. When it appeared that plans weren't falling into place, they either signaled him to get rid of you so you would be the noncommunicating suspect or he just got greedy and decided to toss you over the cliff, make it look like an accident, and take the money. Which, of course, he knew about."

"Then how," Kile asked, "did the money end up with Carlo's courteous little group?"

"Think back," Montoya said, handing him some photographs. "Does this man look familiar?"

"No."

"He was the men's room attendant at Los Arcos. Had been a petty thief but pretty much straightened out. He must have seen the money or been tipped off. We think he got into your room somehow, took the stuff, and was later intercepted by Carlo and killed. Or by someone under Carlo's influence. Incidentally, Mr. Kile, do you have any idea where it is? It does belong to Heritage, or rather its investors.

"Your grandfather knew,...Montoya...What is your first name anyway?"

"I may tell you when this is all over. Please go on."

"One of the last things he told me was that it was safe and that it would be delivered....No, maybe he said he'd take me to it. Shit, I can't remember. Any of you want a drink?"

Kile reached for the bottle, this time using a glass, and poured for himself. "Sure?" he asked again.

"I'll have one with you," Vargas said, handing him a glass from the bed table. "Incidentally, where was the money first hidden?"

"My room, in the box springs. One more thing," Kile said. "Zabata was my friend when I desperately needed one. How can I help?"

chapter
twenty

Calloused as he was by now to abrupt changes in his lifestyle, Clayton Kile still couldn't believe what they wanted him to do. He was also concerned whether he could do it and if he really wanted to. "You are out of your mind," he'd said. "Kile," Montoya had countered, "what you have been through and how you handled those situations totally new to you, leaves no doubt in my mind that you can handle whatever confrontations this project creates."

"We'll give you a crash course," the DEA man had said.

"There are facilities at my ranch," Vargas had added.

"I don't like you," Kile had said to the DEA man. "I don't even know your name, nor have I ever seen any kind of identification."

"Get in line. I'm not paid to be liked. See, you're thinking like us already. And my name is Clarence Harvey. Harv, for obvious reasons, is sufficient." He'd then displayed his government identification and supplemental Mexican credentials. The others had done the same. Montoya's was unique, and Kile observed that his name was Luis Tlaxcala Montoya. He was not only a policeman, he was cadre to a presidential team of specialists formed for combating drugs in Mexico.

"Sleep on it," Harv had suggested as the group left.

"Consider the charges against you that are still pending," Montoya had thrown in, compounding Kile's overloaded considerations.

Kile, after an hour of cursory deliberation, knew he would not be able to sleep. He got up from the bed and walked to the window. Peering at the vague delineations of the vast Copper Canyon, he suddenly laughed, then said aloud, "They are right to one extent; I am not the same person." He remembered someone saying they would talk to Rosa or the inspector about the guard. Stepping to the door, he called out and turned the knob. There was no answer; the door opened to an empty hallway.

There were a few people around the fireplace having nightcaps and discussing the beauty of Copper Canyon. Kile did not want that kind of company.

As he stepped onto the main verandah, he heard her call. "Clay? It is you, isn't it?"

"I'm not sure if it is," he said, turning toward the carved double doors. He smiled and added, "Hello, partner. Recovered?"

"I'm not sure if I'll ever be the same either." Meliss put her arms around his waist, moved her hands up his back, and squeezed. "Hug me back, please," she whispered.

He responded and replied, "You've been through hell, lady, and come out a winner."

She broke first and kissed him lightly. "Feel like a walk?"

"I don't know. The last time I did that some asshole tried to push me off a cliff."

Meliss laughed. "Clay, you never used language like that. Shame on you."

"Maybe that was part of my problem. Let's walk."

As they neared the observation deck, she took hold of his arm. "I'm sorry there was a problem, Clay. Back then, I mean. But you have to…"

"We don't," he interrupted, "have to talk about it. Jesus Christ, that was years ago."

"It wasn't easy on me either."

"Look; I was inadequate, I was selfish, and you were totally inconsiderate!"

"Look yourself, I never set myself up as a sex therapist. Maybe I was selfish, too. I didn't want any binding relationship but you…my god, you…"

"Hey, so I was an asshole. That Clayton Kile is dead, Meliss. And so is the CPA wizard. Nothing seems mathematical anymore. I liked the clean, uninvolved life of financial records. I hated arguing, economic debates, and budget conferences. That's one of the reasons I didn't want, or get, management promotions."

"You also didn't want to understand me, or my lifestyle. Oh god, Clay, what are we doing to each other? Are the scars that deep? Can't what we've been through together wipe out those old feelings? I can't say I love you, Clay, but there's no man in the world I respect more or appreciate more than you. I do love you for what you did. You were my hero. It seems a little stupid now—that wild session, I mean. But I needed it. I was scared of dying. May sound strange, or trite, but your loving me then gave me…well, it gave me the courage to face death without coming apart and collapsing into some kind of hysteria."

"They told me you were dead, you know. That they'd sent someone to kill you. I didn't believe them. I didn't want to. Carlo and Mosquera were trying to kill me. They'd shot

Zabata, and when I realized there were to be no witnesses, I began to think they might not be lying. What did happen?"

"When the old woman woke me and I knew you were gone, I was angry and hurt. She couldn't speak English, but I understood she wanted me out of there. I think she may have been the one who took care of me after my fall. How she got there I have no idea; it's a long way. But it seemed like she was deeply concerned. I don't know, maybe she felt she owed me one...you know, letting Carlo lure me off. Kidnapping might be more appropriate. Anyway, she hid me somewhere in a ravine, returned later, waited until I woke up, and led me back. I didn't know until after they found me—it was Mr. Vargas's group—that someone had been killed near the hut. I knew why you left, Clay, after what Vargas said about the army being after you. From what I learned later and what you've just told me, the woman saved my life." Meliss shuddered and moved toward Clay. "I'm getting chilled. Let's go back." She put her arm through his.

Kile accepted the gesture. "Our past relationship doesn't bother me anymore. I used to shut it out, but it no longer matters. My actions were probably a built-in defense mechanism wanting to lash back."

Meliss said nothing until they reached the verandah. "Clay, have you wondered if it would it be different now? Without the stress and atmosphere of the cave, I mean?"

"No," he lied, "and I don't think I want to find out. Not tonight anyway. Where's your room? I'll see you home."

Reaching the door to his room, Kile knew he'd been unfeeling and abrupt. He regretted the coolness as he'd said goodnight.

Without turning on the lights, he stretched across the bed. Am I subconsciously worried about it, he thought, or do I just have a lot on my mind? It was not easy to concentrate. Things had been immediately demanding, and deliberation was now somehow foreign. Or was it Meliss? She would be no different once things were even slightly normal and she was again

in command of her lifestyle.
　Whether it was the wisp of moonlight shining through the window that drew his attention to the table or that he was thinking of a drink—but there it was, the crystal. An immediate examination assured him it was not the same one but surely from the same cluster. How they delivered it he did not know. There was no question that it came from them. For what purpose? A token of thanks? He didn't know, but he felt a sense of sureness and well-being. He held the faceted piece of quartz for several minutes then, knowing what he wanted to do, set it down, and left the room.
　"Clay?" she asked.
　"Yes." The door opened.
　"Come in, damn you."
　"Just for a minute. I had to clear the air. We've been through too damn much together for me to let...I was rude and I suppose..."
　"You wanted to punish me? Well you did. You got even. I was angry and hurt. Now kiss me, damn it, before I get angry and hurt again."
　It was a different kind of frantic this time, Kile thought, as they kissed and he felt the flush of her cheeks, not an escape, a very real need.
　"I was hoping you'd come," she whispered. "I wanted you so intensely I was ready to knock on your door and beg." She tore at his shirt.
　"Hey, easy," Kile said. "We've got all night." His hands worked down to her hips and pulled the warmth of her body closer. It was different, he realized, as he relaxed to her feverish aggression.
　Something initially satisfied, Meliss pulled away, removed her robe and, standing naked, said, "Whatever you want, however you want it, I'm ready, Clayton Kile."
　Kile enjoyed the feeling of seeing her slender body with long legs apart, hands on hips, small breasts swollen and nipples erect. It was a body that had once been his nemesis.

No, it hadn't been the body; it was her open and forthright attitude that debilitated him. She had shown an initiative that, in his insular experience, was totally foreign. The recollection passed quickly, and there were no problems. He again drew her into his arms. "You are the most sensual woman I've ever seen," he said, kissing and nibbling at her neck.

"Get on the bed, Clay." Her voice had a raspy softness. "I'm going to interrogate your body."

"Let's improvise," he said, as she slid in beside him. Vigorously, tenderly, and sometimes experimentally, they loved...always pausing when it became intense and, when there was no holding back, yielding and collapsing, wet, exhausted, satisfied.

There was a bond there, Kile realized in the predawn hour, that was more than sexual or physical. When she stirred, then moved against him, he wanted her again. She eagerly responded. Later they slept, bodies spoon fashion.

Kile was about to enter his room when he heard the voice of Captain Rosa. "Señor Kile, one moment please." It was half-past nine. "The chief inspector wishes to see you."

"Clayton Kile," the inspector said, when they entered what had been the command post, "you are aware that you are still in custody, are you not?" Kile nodded. "And your freedom is based on your word of honor not to attempt another escape?"

Again Kile nodded, then said, "What seems to be the problem, Chief Inspector?"

"Even though you will probably be exonerated of any and all murder charges, you will have to be tried on the escape from custody. Government levels above me insist on it. There was a great deal of activity on the part of local forces and the army contingent. They want something to show for it. There were, after all, seven murders."

"You have got to be kidding, Inspector. What about the arrangements with DEA and your..."

"Kile, I never 'kid,' as you put it. Nor have I ever joked

about official matters in my twenty-seven years in this work. Your government's agency and our liaison have no say in the matter. Because of the public nature of all this, you will be transported to Chihuahua for trial." The inspector turned to his captain. "You will expedite, Rosa. We do not want to go through some embarrassing situation again. Is that clear?"

"Of course, Commander," Rosa said as he saluted.

"Would it be possible to speak with Harvey or Montoya?" Kile asked.

"I will advise them of the changes," the inspector said. "You will be allowed to pack, but do so quickly."

"What the hell is going on here?" Harv asked, as he and Montoya arrived at the jeep which was to transport Kile and two officers to the train.

"For security," Kile said, holding up his manacled wrists.

"We have a message about the money, Kile," Montoya said, seeming to ignore the situation. "A puzzling sort of communication."

"I still want to know what this goddamn outfit is up to?" Clarence Harvey was not diplomatic.

"I have to stand trial for the escape—orders from higher up. Listen, will one of you locate Meliss Cortland and..."

"Kile," Montoya interrupted, "I said we had word about the missing bonds."

"Where's Rosa and the inspector?" Harv yelled. "Don't leave until I talk to them."

The two officers ignored him and told the driver to start the vehicle.

Montoya, in uniform, stepped in front of the jeep and gave an order in Spanish. The driver shrugged and turned off the key.

"As I said," Montoya continued, "we received a message that the package of importance, belonging to the North American, was safe, and that he would know where it was hidden. Make any sense?"

"Not that I can think of now," Kile lied. "But it looks as

though I'll have plenty of time to think about it. Will you please get a message to Meliss? She wasn't in her room a few minutes ago."

"Of course. Harv and I will get on this trial thing immediately, be assured of that. The whole thing is ridiculous, a stupid waste of time and money."

"Pardon, Officer Montoya," one of the guards said, "but we must get Señor Kile to the train now. It has been so ordered."

"I understand, go on. I am sorry for the delay and will so advise your commander if there is a problem."

The jeep proceeded down the drive as Montoya yelled, "I'll talk to Miss Cortland, don't worry."

"Tell her about the message," Kile called out. The jeep moved down the driveway and out of sight.

chapter
twenty-one

The trial of Clayton Kile could have set a record for expediency. On the fourth day of incarceration, the guard led him to a windowless interview room and told him to sit. Twenty minutes later a man in a suit entered and announced, "*Su abogado*, Señor Kile, your lawyer." He went on to explain he was a consultant for the task force, had been a police officer, and was a friend of Lieutenant Montoya.

"The officer from La Paz?" Kile asked. "Luis T. Montoya?"

"The same. He was promoted two days ago. I do not have much time, so I'll be brief, and probably abrupt. Agencies of our respective governments have, within their limitations, been at work. Incidentally, I can not actually represent you, I am here to explain the options. Considering certain political and administrative pressures—ego trips, actually—there are limits to leniency. You can agree to the charge and be sentenced tomorrow, or not agree and wait for trial."

"Doesn't give me much choice."

"You were in custody, Clayton Kile, and you did escape."

"How long would it take for a trial?"

"Not to impress you with worry, Señor, but I will be the first to admit our system is notorious for delays in criminal justice. You must remember we are under Napoleonic Law and a man is guilty until proven innocent."

"What kind of sentence are we talking about? Not that it would seem to make much difference."

"That is presently being researched and considered. It will be announced tomorrow."

Kile chuckled, causing a frown on his visitor's face. "I'm sorry, Counselor, it's just that…there's a great deal of irony here that I can't explain. Do you know anything about me, my past or profession?"

"Nothing, except that you are a friend of Lieutenant Montoya and your recent past has been complicated."

Again Kile chuckled. "I suppose that sums it up. Do I have time to think about it?"

"No. I must know now, as the wheels are in motion. Understand, however, there are pressures for leniency."

In his mind Kile saw a crystal. "Tell them I'll plead guilty and throw myself upon the mercy of the court."

The lawyer smiled. "An American cliché in crime cinema is it not? It will be done tomorrow."

It was not until the interpreter advised he'd been sentenced to one year in prison that Kile accepted the reality of the tribunal. While the judge continued in Spanish, Kile again searched for someone he might recognize. He was hoping he'd see Meliss. "You will be transported," the interpreter continued, "to a work facility yet to be determined."

Sounds better than prison, Kile thought, as he was led back to his communal quarters. There was a disappointment that neither the American nor Montoya had been in contact.

That he had been tried and sentenced so quickly gave him sudden celebrity status. Those who understood were sure he had done much more than alleged but had connections. The fact that he would only serve one year did not matter. One of the more articulate proceeded to teach him Spanish, explaining it would be of great help in securing the easier tasks.

At noon he was again led to the judicial chambers. "For photographs," he was told. Thinking it would be some kind of prison record thing, he was surprised that it became a series of poses with guards leading him from the room.

At three in the afternoon he was again led out. This time it was an office. As he was being unshackled, a familiar voice sounded. "Ah, Kile, it is good to see you, my friend."

"What kept you, Montoya, or should I say Lieutenant?"

"So you heard. I am sorry about not getting here sooner. Not that I could have done anything."

"It would have helped, having someone in the wings."

"Come, sit here at this desk while I explain. It will not be what you think." Montoya talked for half an hour, telling how the sentence would ultimately be commuted, that providing things go well he could be pardoned and that the photographs were for publicity. "More about that later," he went on. "Right now we shall get you out of here, get you cleaned up and rested."

"I could use...do you know how long it's been since I had a good steak?"

It was three hours and dinner before Kile was able to glean more information from Montoya. "The simplest first, please, the photos?"

"We want Mosquera and his spy network to know you have been convicted and put away. As we told you, our being able to identify him is limited to..." Montoya stopped as both he and Kile realized their error.

"Good god, you're protecting me and she's...where is she anyway?"

"Didn't she come to see you? She's supposed to be here in Chihuahua. Left the day after...or was it...she had to get some camera work done here and then do a photojournal thing on one of Pancho Villa's alleged widows. I told her, after giving her your message, how she could see you. Excuse me, I've got to do some checking. Go back to your room at the hotel when you finish. I'll contact you later. Remember, you are in my custody. Screw up and you're gone forever."

"Can't I help?"

"Not in Chihuahua."

"Well then, *buena suerte, amigo.*"

Montoya looked back, grinned, and said, "I should have told you prison was an education."

It was daylight when Kile heard a waking rap on his door. "Yes, who...*quién?*"

"It's Montoya, Clayton. Open quickly, the news is not good." Kile opened to a bleary-eyed cop. "God, you look awful."

"No time for discussion. Get dressed. You are needed."

Fifteen minutes later, in a cab crossing the plaza, Kile said, "Okay, Lieutenant, you've evaded long enough. What is it?"

"She is dead, my friend. I am sorry. The body was found two days ago."

There was heavy silence, then, "You're certain about this?"

"Reasonably so, but you will have to confirm the identity. That's why I said you were needed. Are you...can you do it?"

"How did it happen?"

"She was either followed or someone in Chihuahua was waiting. Their network is extensive, you know. I..."

"Damn it, how did it happen?"

"Gunshot, three times, once in the head, the other two in the chest. Someone came to her hotel room. She apparently opened the door and caught three 9 mm rounds. The perpetrator then closed the door and left. That's the way it looked, according to the investigation. Must have used a silencer as no one heard shots. Clayton, we can wait. There are others that could identify the..."

"No, let's get it over with, have to make it final."

"Do you know her family?"

Kile did not answer until the taxi stopped at the morgue and Montoya again asked, "Did you know her relatives?"

"As far as I know there was only a sister. No, I believe she had some cousins in Northern California. The sister lived in Denver. You have to remember, Luis, until La Paz I hadn't seen Meliss in four years."

"The sister's name?"

"The same, Courtland. Unless she married in the last few years. Her first name is Gwen. That's all I can give you. Oh, she worked for the state government. Legal secretary, if I remember correctly."

They entered the building and proceeded down an echoing corridor that amplified voices and footsteps to irritating decibels. "Let's stop here a minute," Montoya said. "I'll notify someone about the sister." He stepped to a counter and carried on a conversation in Spanish.

Pausing at double doors in the right wing, Montoya hesitated. "I have to go in with you; they don't know you and the identification must be witnessed."

When the cover was pulled back, Kile swallowed against the dryness in his throat, looked at Montoya, and nodded, then turned and walked out.

Montoya signed something and followed. "Coffee?"

Again Kile nodded.

The second cup was also taken in silence as they sat in an uncrowded cafe a block away. Then, as though reading his partner, Luis asked, "Were you in love with her?"

There was a continued silence then, "Oh, I'm sorry, I was trying to put things in perspective....It won't work. I don't know, I suppose I was. At least that was the way I saw it years ago. What we went through up there...I think we each saw someone entirely different. You know, facets we didn't know we had. Right now I don't know what I feel. Too much went on up there and I'm not the same person I was. Do you know I'd never fired a pistol before? Up there I killed three men and...well, right now it doesn't bother me much. Luis, it's a wonder I didn't crack. More things happened to me in one week than in my entire life, violent, traumatic things. I amazed myself. Not at the time—there was too much going on—but then later I would think, did I actually do that? Was that really me? Is it a case of emotional overload and burnout, and feelings are no longer there?"

The lieutenant looked directly at Kile. "You are not some erratic freak. That is exactly why we felt you could be of help. The fact that you survived such happenings without...how is your expression?...without coming apart at the joints is not some quirk. It was you, Clayton Kile, as you always have been. It is not known how someone will react to certain kinds of incidents until a situation actually tests them. Do you want a couple of days? Before we start your training, or should I say sentence?"

"No, let's get on with it. Where do we begin?"

"Barranca Divisadero, Copper Canyon. There is still the matter of some money and bonds that concerns your government. Then to a secluded and highly secure training center for your crash course."

"Something I'd like to know. Do you suspect some kind of leak in your task force, or the police agencies?"

"Yes, there is always that problem when so much money floats around and pay is low. You, Señor Kile, are going to help us find out who it is."

chapter
twenty-two

The camp was not a joint operation. DEA contributed funds and instructors. Agents from the United States were given special courses when assigned to Latin American areas. It was this situation and the wishes of the task force of Mexico that allowed entry of Clayton Kile. He would be trained, in one week, for a specific assignment. The camp commander and chief of instruction did not like the arrangement. "Lieutenant Montoya," he said, after Kile had been introduced, indoctrinated, and ushered off to his quarters, "is this man a thrill-seeking soldier of fortune type or is he on some kind of revenge crusade?"

"Neither, Colonel Vergado, although he was a friend of my grandfather and feels the loss as I do."

"What about the Courtland woman?"

"They had been in a relationship some years ago. They were hardly speaking when I first saw them in La Paz. But, apparently, the ordeals they suffered together brought them close again. It is not a thing to be concerned about, I assure you."

"He has not had law enforcement training of any kind?"

"That is correct, Colonel, but I feel I know the man. He has handled extreme situations as well as most of our graduates. He is, believe me, a natural. Let me give you some examples." Montoya spent the next thirty minutes detailing Kile's activities, concentrating on the man's initiative and the resourcefulness. "And," he said in closing, "we can not identify Mosquera, code name El Fantasmo, without him. The others are all dead."

"If he is so trustworthy," the colonel asked, "why such secrecy surrounding his recovery of the money and negotiable securities?"

Montoya took a deep breath, then said, "Neither his government nor ours was concerned with where it was. Getting it back was the important thing."

"And you let him, a prisoner in your custody, go wandering in the barranca by himself?"

"Colonel, there are three reasons why we let that happen. One, part of the push for prosecution was to get him involved—I hope to god he never figures that out—so trusting him was important. Two, where would he go?"

"But you just explained how resourceful he was and he was loose with a considerable amount of money."

"As I was about to say, Colonel, the third reason has to do with the fact that it was very important to him to find it and avoid extradition and prosecution in his own country for theft, embezzlement, absconding, or whatever it would be."

"Still, I do not like loose ends. The fact that he is a prisoner here, in the midst of a highly secret training organization, bothers me considerably."

"There is one other thing, Colonel, the safekeeping was entrusted to a shaman and his council. The repository, I believe, was in a sacred grotto and...well, you know the importance of these things."

"They don't want us to know, but allow a damned gringo to wander all over their territory."

"They obviously trust him, don't they?"

"That's another matter that shows there's more to this man. What's his connection with the Tarahumara?"

"I don't know, sir, and I haven't asked. I accept that he was befriended by my grandfather, and that's sufficient. Remember, he is now in a position of trust among the canyon people that few of us have."

"Yes, Montoya, I forgot for a moment that you have a long line of ancestral ties there. Now, I must be going, I have a lecture to give." He exited with Montoya holding the door. "Lieutenant, I will try to keep an open mind. No special or lenient consideration, however. Understood?"

"Quite clear, sir. And remember, he does want that full pardon."

By the third day Kile had convinced the colonel he was neither on an ego trip nor pathologically thirsting for vengeance. That evening Montoya visited headquarters from another section of the ranch. "Good evening, sir. Señor Kile is doing well, is he not?"

"Do come in, Lieutenant. You know damn well he is. If he were in better shape physically, and that only comes with lengthy conditioning, and if he knew Spanish..."

"He would be one of our top trainees."

"Precisely, Montoya. According to the range officer, he is—as you put it—a natural. He's outshooting those here for refresher courses."

"How about the forced language thing?"

"Except for interpreting in matters of instruction and, of course, safety, he is on his own. Has to use his phrase book or he is ignored. This works surprisingly well during meals."

"And the evening language tutoring?"

"I found some time ago that an intense and condensed course, such as we are doing for him, does not penetrate after a strenuous day. So Señor Kile does his two hours early, before physical training. But we are not magicians and he is a gringo, so all we can accomplish, hopefully, is enough vocabulary and phrases to keep him out of trouble. And, of course, ask questions. Would you like a drink, Luis?"

"No, thank you, Colonel, I have a training mission to lead at midnight. Not that I feel it would affect me, but it is not good leadership for the men to smell liquor on their lieutenant. You know, sir, all I want this course to do for Kile is help keep him alive. They definitely want him dead. The murder of the Courtland woman proves that."

"I understand, of course. He's safe here. It will be your problem once you embark."

"His problem, sir. Remember, he will be on his own much of the time. Goodnight, sir. Thank you for seeing me."

"Goodnight, Luis. Check daily if you can."

Two days later Kile was called in from a simulated raid to be greeted by Montoya and Harv.

"I was beginning to think my own government had forsaken me. It is Harv, isn't it?" The DEA man nodded.

"Luis, so I don't have to take the time to look it up, what the hell does *tiburón* mean?"

"Ever hear of a town near San Francisco called Tiburón?"

"Yes."

"It's Spanish for shark. Why do you ask?" The men moved from the verandah into the one-story structure that served as HQ.

Kile chuckled. "That's what I was called when we were briefed on the raid, '*el tiburón*.'"

Harv, frowning, said, "I hope that isn't some indication of a feeding frenzy when you get involved in the real thing."

"Perhaps they are in awe of your being so cool," Montoya interjected.

"Yeah," said Harv, "or uneasy about what that stoic reserve really covers."

"Clarence," Kile said with emphasis, "I still find it difficult to like you."

"As I said before, I'm not paid to be liked."

"Gentlemen, please," Montoya said, "let's not forget why we are meeting."

For an hour Kile was briefed by Montoya and Harv on what was known of El Fantasma and the corridor plan. Although not finalized, some indication of the proposed strategy was also discussed. Mosquera, as he was known by Kile, was the Ghost; he was unknown, in a physical sense, to any of the agencies. His drug trade logistical accomplishments, however, were legendary. The fact that little or nothing was known about him and that combined intelligence organizations could not come up with anything, was frustrating to say the least. "Any questions or comments?" Luis asked near the end of the hour.

"Mosquera did not seem at all magical," Kile said, "or the least bit formidable, in my contact with him. Are you sure we are talking about the same man?"

"We do have names," Harv answered, "a lot of them, and one is Mosquera. The fact that he was in Copper Canyon, had some kind of organization and accomplices, which included a spy network, and obviously was not developing a tour guide agency, pretty much tells us it's him."

"He's not much of a judge of men if those two idiots in the…in the canyon were any indication." Kile had almost mentioned the cave. "It seems he would have more stalwart assistants."

"They could have been pickups here in the Sierra Madre, part of his developing manpower." Harv paused, then continued, "It is thought, by our analysts, that he may deliberately avoid permanent relationships, either on a personal level or that of the drug trade, as part of his mystique and self-preservation."

"I don't quite understand this corridor thing," Kile said. "Why go to all this trouble when, from what I've read and learned here, they crash land planes in the Florida swamps, run half-million dollar yachts onto the beach, and create their own banks? Why do they want to screw around in the Sierra Madre?"

Lieutenant Luis Montoya grinned. "We have wondered that same thing. Our conclusion is shaky, but here it is: One, it could simply be a diversion, forcing our task force and the DEA to spread out and weaken effectiveness. Two, as things have tightened up considerably in the southeastern states, it is both an alternative route and a staging area for delayed delivery. Also, it has come to our attention that it included plans for growing areas at different levels of the barranca. You see, Kile, and this is speculation, the canyon is almost tropical in the lower levels where there is water. The fact that it is remote and vast makes policing aspects most difficult."

"One more thing," Harv added. "From the canyon they could route north into Texas or Arizona, they could go west into the gulf, and ship north toward the California border. With traffic at Tijuana, for example, any number could get through with small amounts. To say nothing of the vast stretches of inadequately manned border."

"I see one conclusion," Kile said. "You need an entire army."

Luis and Harv looked at each other and smiled triumphantly. It was the first time Kile had seen Clarence Harvey do anything but frown. Harv turned and said, "Bingo! You've got the big picture. And you got it before burnout or the impotence of frustration."

Kile shrugged. "I have three more days. What then?"

"Montoya runs the show," Harv said. "I'm just available."

"As I said earlier, we are monitoring Acapulco, Mazatlán, Topolobampo, and Guaymas as marine contact probables. We will fly you into the most likely port and, as things change, jump you around."

"It just occurred to me," Kile said, "aren't my description and sketches sufficient?"

"I must have neglected to tell you." Montoya sounded apologetic. "Mosquera apparently uses disguises. We feel you should, in view of your contact with him, be able to sense his identity through any deception. You can see why you are so important to us."

"Another thought just occurred to me, gentlemen."

"And that is?" Luis asked.

"I'll also be a decoy, won't I?"

Without hesitation or surprise, Montoya answered, "Not in the primary sense, not at all. That El Fant...that Mosquera wants you dead is no secret, or have you forgotten?"

The urge not to be involved kept pushing up from Kile's past. Then, as he thought of Zabata and Meliss, it vanished.

"No, I haven't. My circuits are still adjusting, that's all."

"Good, my friend, then we shall see you in three days."

In the evening, returning from dinner, Kile saw Vargas leaving HQ. It was the first time he'd seen him since being transported to Chihuahua. "Señor Vargas," he called out. "*Un momento, por favor.*" I wonder if he heard me, Kile thought, as the man disappeared around the north side of the building. There was the whinny of a horse, then hoofbeats. A man on a pinto rode from behind the structure and disappeared into the grove of pinion that spread for several acres north of camp. Well, he does have a ranch to run, Kile thought, as he continued to his quarters.

At breakfast the following morning, Kile, seated next to his language tutor, said, "I saw Señor Vargas last night, does he come around often?"

"Occasionally," the man answered. "He has many interests to maintain and operate. In fact, he is now on his way to the logging area, according to the commandant. Why do you ask?"

"Look, I know of his involvement, so..."

"I don't know of any involvement other than he has allowed the operation of our training center on his ranch. He lost two sons to drugs. One is in prison for transporting; the other is dead from an overdose. Señor Vargas is very much against the marketing and the use of any controlled substance. You will be leaving soon, is that not true?"

"I'm not sure," Kile said, thinking, I can play their game as well as they can. "I'm here for an indefinite period."

"But a highly accelerated period, that I know."

"Yes. If you will excuse me, I have surveillance techniques this morning."

"*Buena suerte.*"

"*Gracias. Adios.*"

"Not bad, Kile, not bad at all."

The following morning, during a mock raid, as Kile hid in the brush waiting for his partner's signal, a muted whack tore at the ground to his right. He dove forward, hitting the ground prone, rolled, and crawled toward the cover of a rocky overhang. There was no report following the impact. He was sure a silencer had been used. He waited. After an estimated two minutes, Kile worked his way to the opposite side of the outcrop. The whang of a second shot, ricocheting off the rock, sent him plunging for cover. "Jesus Christ," he muttered. "And I'm not even through training."

After a cautious wait, he was about to try another movement when he heard his partner yell, "Kile, where the hell are you? The instructor is impatient, and pissed."

"Stay down, my friend," Kile answered. "Someone's taking pot shots at me."

"If it's you, and only you," his partner said as he carefully worked his way to Kile's position, "then I don't have to worry, do I?"

"Thanks a lot, asshole. I suggest you don't test that theory."

With the arrival of the training exercise monitor, it was assumed the suspect had fled, but a search was immediately ordered. Kile and his partner were told to probe for the bullet that struck first.

"It looks like a .38," the partner said, as he extricated the copper and lead missile from a hastily dug furrow. "But probably a .357."

"How long will they search?" Kile asked.

"Until dark at least. This is one hell of a blow to the security of what we are doing here."

"It could be one of our own people and that would make any search a waste of time, wouldn't it?"

"That's impossible," the partner said. "We are intensely screened and carefully selected." Kile did not mention the probability of an informant within the camp, or at least inside the task force. He had begun to understand internal security. "I don't know the area, but it seems to me finding the suspect will be almost impossible."

"Agreed, and I also anticipate an all-night perimeter watch. They'll call it training. Let's walk on over to HQ and give our report."

After being interrogated for some time, Kile was told to remain in the building. "Someone will be sent for your personal belongings," an aide said. "Montoya has been informed and will arrive in two hours. They obviously want you out of here."

"I'll sleep for a while then. Is there a room with a cot?"

"Of course, Señor Kile, but first you must be armed. Which of the pistols you have used do you prefer?"

"An automatic, 9 mm, please. Like the one used at the range."

"And the holster?"

"Waist, inside model. I'm not comfortable with a shoulder setup."

"I'll be back in a few minutes. Then you can rest."

Sluggish at first, Kile was fully alert by the time the helicopter lifted off. "We'll talk later," Montoya had said.

Kile no longer pondered the happenings of the past weeks. Nor did he reflect on his own changes. The ability to shut things off seemed natural.

"We'll land at Chihuahua," Luis said, as they veered northeast, "and change to conventional aircraft, a small one. We can talk then."

Kile nodded. Then, as the chopper skimmed a ridge…his intuitive sense of danger was too late…an explosive impact sent the chopper into an erratic whirl. The sound of rushing air seemed oddly pleasant. The machine went into a second loop, and Kile knew it would not complete a third. There was a brief feeling of suspension as it stalled then plunged into the high branches of thick ponderosa and careened onto a dense thicket of brush. Stunned, trapped, semiconscious, Kile waited for the explosive fire.

chapter
twenty-three

The fire did erupt, but in a minor burst of flame that spread through what remained of the fuselage. The first impact must have done something to the fuel supply, Kile thought, realizing he had a chance. This rush of survival instinct stimulated the strength to twist his way loose. The pilot was dead. Luis Montoya, his right arm bent the wrong way, was unconscious. I know he's alive, Kile thought, he's bleeding. The careless speed in which he got himself and Montoya out was unnecessary, he realized, after dragging his friend through the maze of underbrush and into a clearing; the fire was dying out.

Got to stop his bleeding, Kile told himself, at least slow it down until I can get back with the medical kit. He ripped the T-shirt from under his camouflage jacket and pressed the wadded fabric against Montoya's arm. Removing his web belt, he bound the temporary bandage, then checked for other wounds. The cursory examination was cut short by a sudden thought; someone would be coming to confirm his death. "Good god," he whispered. "They could be here anytime." He knew it would depend on where they fired from. Weapons and the kit were vital.

Kile tore his way through the brush—it seemed thicker—and fought upward to the wreckage. He was becoming aware of his own injuries. The automatic rifle was damaged and inoperative. He didn't try the flashlight, but stuck it in his waistband. Don't want to give them a signal, he thought, as he searched for Montoya's pistol. In seconds he had it and the pilot's revolver. Unable to find any additional ammo, he worked his way to what had been a compartment and pulled out his bag. Stuffing pistols and the medical canister inside, he secured the zipper and began threading his way back to Montoya.

The course was worth it, he thought, as he checked his first aid on Montoya. Can't take time to splint the arm just yet, got other priorities. Luis made a groaning sound and began to mumble. Kile broke the ammonia capsule and held it under Montoya's nose. "Can you hear me?" he asked. "Luis, listen...try to understand....They are going to be here. They are going to finish us off unless...goddamn it, Luis." Montoya opened his eyes, mumbled again, and sank back into the refuge of unconsciousness.

Laying out the weapons, Kile took stock of his defenses: Two automatics and one revolver, a .357. Both clips and the cylinder full. He laid out the two extra clips taken from Montoya's belt and one speed loader found on the pilot. Knowing metallic sound would carry, he carefully checked the action on his three pistols. Satisfied they were operational, he searched through his bag for the box of shells; he wanted them handy. Emptying the box into his fatigue breast pockets, he reached back into the case and pulled out the crystal. I guess Vargas was right, Kile mused, it sure as hell changed my life. He set it on a slab of limestone that edged the clearing and turned to check on Montoya. As he did, his peripheral vision caught a flash of reflected light in the crystal. "They're here," he whispered and crawled toward Luis. "Montoya...listen, someone's coming, and it's not a rescue team. Don't try to respond, just listen. I'm leaving your pistol here in your hand and putting a clip back in your belt. I know it's the wrong hand, but it will have to do. I'm going to crawl outside the clearing and find out how many there are. I'm hoping they think we're still in the wreckage. Don't do anything to call attention to where you are. If you hear firing you'll have to figure your own strategy. I'll yell if I can direct your fire. Otherwise...well, *amigo, buena suerte.*"

There was a barely audible response, "*Cuidado, Tiburon,* I will do as you say."

Kile covered Montoya's chest with a windbreaker to conceal the pistol, moved all items out of sight, and disappeared into the matted brush.

Concealed, but able to see the crash site and the clearing, Kile heard them. He was thankful for the crash course in Spanish.

"Hello, are you in need of help? We have come to help you." There was silence. Then, in a quieter voice, "I think they are all dead, Señor." Kile could not make out what was said by an even lower voice, but was sure of it being some kind of instruction. He observed two lights go on, beams searching the wreckage area, as men worked their way down. They were about twenty yards apart. Another light came on, downhill, below the site, and fifty yards to the south. That's three, Kile figured, and the one giving directions makes four. Unless there's more than one with each light.

A voice again called out, "We are here to help you, where are you? We have medicine." The sound came from somewhere between the lights on the slope and the one to the south. That's five, Kile counted. I can get the first three once they converge on the crash site. The others will draw in on my muzzle flash so I'll have to shoot fast and move. I'll need cover. Damn, that light downslope, they'll walk right into the clearing. I should have dragged Luis into some cover, too damn late now.

"I am sure they are all dead, Señor." It was the same voice, one of the two light carriers. "The brush is very thick here. It will take time getting to the crash." A different voice, from high on the ridge, answered, "Get as close as you can and..."

Kile did not understand the rest of the order but was sure of one thing—it was Mosquera!

"Watch out for the men below you," Mosquera added, as two lights closed in.

Montoya, I hope you keep your cool. Kile was amused by his thought. He's the professional, and I'm telling him to keep cool. Kile judged the distance to the helicopter to be about thirty yards from his position, close enough for accurate fire. He would hit the dual lights first, then swing on the single.

The duel staccato of machine-gun fire and muzzle blast obliterated the silence of the mountain and lighted the area with strobe-like flashes.

"The bastards are saturating the chopper," Kile muttered. "They aren't taking any chances." Without thinking about it, he sighted on the lone flashlight and got off four rounds. The flashlight dropped to the ground and rolled, disappearing in ground cover. The rapid firing was over in seconds and he heard the two gunmen conversing. They were going to reload; one was to hold the light. In rapid fire, Kile emptied the weapon, rolled to his right, changed to the revolver, and got off six more rounds before diving for better cover. Waiting, he inserted another clip in the automatic, reloaded the revolver, and assured himself he would be ready.

Mosquera called to his men. There was a response from an area directly above the chopper debris. No sounds came from near the site or south below it. Got three of them at least, Kile calculated. That leaves two, maybe three. The big question is, how many more machine guns? Kile removed the flashlight from his waistband, covered the lens, and tested it. It worked. Stretching out to his left he reached toward a forked limb in some brush growing from an outcrop. Wedging the light securely, he ripped off the lower half of his pant leg. Cutting half into strips, he produced a three-foot length which he tied to the remaining half. He could hear faint conversation drifting from the upper slope. Again reaching out, he covered the lens carefully and pushed the switch. Only a minimal amount of light showed, and it was toward the ground. Withdrawing behind his cover, he slowly pulled at slack in his line. He was aware of chest pains. Raising slightly, he aimed his pistol toward the area above the helicopter and pulled off the cover. The sound and the flash were like magnets for the five rounds he sent uphill. The light was no longer working. There was a return burst of fire from farther up the ridge, then silence, followed by cursing in Spanish.

I think his gun jammed, Kile told himself, as he rushed for the chute between vertical strata, and there is no more action from my target area. Four down, one or two to go—and one of them is Mosquera.

As Kile worked his way up the partially filled chute, the emerging quarter moon made things more visible. He was sure now that if any of them started down it would be right past his goal, another twenty yards up. Any other way would, as far as he could see, be difficult and dangerous.

He heard the man stumble, then swear, as small rocks rolled down the slope. Kile was not quite to his destination, but paused, then raised to peer over the small escarpment. There he was, not more than ten yards away—Mosquera. "Freeze, you son of a bitch, or you're a dead man." Kiles voice was even and firm. "Where are the others?"

"There are no others, Señor Kile, I assure you."

"I want your arms stretched high. You will drop the pistol. Now, damn it! That's it, now do a three-sixty, turn...slowly." The way Mosquera craned his neck as he moved indicated he was not sure where Kile was.

"You are not a stupid man, *amigo*, so why don't you come where real fortunes are made? My people would welcome a man with your talents. Say one hundred thousand down and..."

"Save it, shithead. I wouldn't trade your life for a million. You murdered two people very close to me."

"You have murdered several of my people. What's the difference?"

He's stalling, Kile reasoned. He's waiting for one of the others. "Look at me, you bastard...here, up to your left."

"You won't shoot me in cold blood. You are a sworn officer and will take me in for questioning and trial."

Kile laughed. "I was to be sworn in tomorrow by both Mexico and the DEA. Your attempts on my life blew that. So I'm just a man defending himself."

"I still say your conscience won't..." The 9 mm slug made a small mark as it entered the forehead, stopping the man in midsentence and removing the back part of his skull.

Clayton Kile dropped below his parapet and waited. He waited to feel something, but there was nothing. He waited for some indication of the others. There were no sounds. Maybe that's all of them, he thought.

After an estimated quarter-hour, Kile started back. He could wait it out no longer and was concerned about Montoya. Moving slowly and pausing for sounds, he grew impatient. He felt like stepping into the first clearing and yelling, "Come get me you bastards." Knowing that would be idiotic and probably his death warrant, he maintained his methodical pace.

Circling to a downhill edge of the clearing, he could see Montoya had not moved. "God, I hope you're not dead," he whispered. He was hesitant to move into the open. There was something....What was it? anxiety, premonition?

A metallic sound in the clear night air answered his question, and a voice said, "I liked you from our first meeting, Señor Kile, and I'm sorry I have to do this. Drop your pistol and move forward please, I have to be sure about the lieutenant."

There was a stab of betrayal and loss as Kile recognized the voice. It was Vargas. "Why?" he asked. "You have everything in the world going for you."

"Ranching and lumbering are hard work and pay very little these days, hardly enough to maintain a decent life."

Got to stall, Kile told himself. "What about your sons?"

"A cover story. They were imbeciles. One is dead, the other is a raving maniac. Remove the cover from Montoya. I don't want to shoot unless I have to. Less sound the better. There is a search party coming over the next ridge, in case you hadn't noticed."

Kile was puzzled. He hadn't covered Montoya's face. "Did you kill Meliss Courtland?"

"What difference does it make? Remove it, now!"

"It was you. That's why she opened the door." Kile squatted and grasped the collar of the jacket covering the face and upper torso of Luis Montoya. He saw the slight movement, pulled, and fell to the side as three rounds entered Vargas's chest. The point-blank sound was deafening. Ears ringing, Kile drew the revolver and turned. Vargas did not move.

"Sorry," Luis said in a dry whisper. "It was the only way I could manage it. Didn't know who was coming." Kile then noticed the knife and sheath on the dead man's belt. "The bastard was going to stab me. Did you have any idea?"

"No, he was not even a suspect."

Light from the approaching helicopter rushed up and down ridges. Voices could be heard.

"Want a steady job, Clayton?"

"You want your other arm broken?"

chapter
twenty-four

"I've just seen x-rays of your foot, Mr. Kile. You may have some permanent damage there, perhaps a limp. You compounded the injury by excessive activity."

"I had things to do, Doctor, sorry."

"The pain must have been intense."

"The ribs bothered me more. How's Lieutenant Montoya?"

"His pain threshold is as amazing as yours. He's doing well, considering we thought we might have to take his arm. There are some internal injuries. He'll be here for some time."

"Where did you train, Doctor...?"

"Morello, Maurice Morello. UC San Francisco. Why do you ask?"

"Your excellent command of English."

"I was raised in the San Francisco Bay area. Came back to Chihuahua because I was needed. Does the cast bother you? Other than itching, I mean."

"No, but breathing is uncomfortable."

The doctor chuckled. "You go through physical hell and don't say a word, according to the emergency crew, and now you find simple breathing painful."

"When can I see Luis?"

"I'll see if we can't have a nurse wheel you down tomorrow. Okay?"

"Fine, thank you. Give him my regards."

A nurse entered, whispered with Dr. Morello as he exited, then gave Kile a shot. "You will sleep well." She left.

When Kile again opened his eyes, it was midmorning. The nurse, a different one, smiled and asked, "You are hungry, no?"

"I am, but also groggy. Do you know Lieutenant Montoya?"

"No, he is not on this section."

Kile ate well, then slept again. He was awake when the evening meal was brought in. "Has anyone asked to see me?" Kile was concerned that there had been no debriefing, no one to discuss his custody status, and no contact from DEA or other agencies—not even from the Mexican government.

The girl smiled and shook her head.

"Okay, I'll try my Spanish. *¿Personas venga aquí para me, a días?*"

The girl giggled and said, "*No, Señor. Lo siento mucho,*" and left.

Clayton Kile was beginning to feel uncomfortable, in an emotional way, until the crux of a camp discussion surfaced. There is a letdown, one of the senior instructors told him, after most operations: "Usually minor, but you should be prepared for it and able to recognize the symptoms. It is sometimes referred to as post-operation syndrome, or anxiety. You see, you have been totally involved—most often in a life and death situation—you've trained for it and you have geared for it. So it is only natural that you and your emotions have to accommodate the body."

Kile refused that night's sleeping pill.

At ten in the morning Kile was helped into a wheelchair and trundled off to his visit with Montoya. Doctor Morello was still present.

Luis managed a smile and said, "Your accommodations acceptable?"

"You look terrible, Lieutenant. Good morning, Doctor."

Morello nodded and continued writing.

"Don't get maudlin with me, *gringo*. By the way, Doctor Morello tells me you could have given me morphine up there. The kit..."

"Yes," Morello interrupted. "It would have been standard procedure. You have been trained, haven't you?"

"Doctor, I needed this man, needed him badly. He was the only possible help I had. I didn't have any idea how extensive his injuries were, but I wanted him responsive if possible. Morphine would have eased the pain but would probably have made him useless—and most likely dead."

"See, Doctor Morello, as I told you, logic and selfishness all the way down the line."

"Why no visiting dignitaries?" Kile asked, after Morello left. "I thought we'd be deluged by now."

"Your own logic would apply, my friend, they want us alert. It's not as though we left loose ends."

"No one was shot in the back, is that it?"

"Don't be defensive, I wasn't implying anything. I had a visitor early this morning."

"Yes?"

"I suppose he is what you would call your probation officer. Your agencies have been pressuring, and he wants to wrap up your status as soon as possible. Before it gets any stickier. Your situation has not pleased many of our government officials. In fact, some have been quite nervous. Anyway, my friend, the sentence will be commuted to your stay here in the hospital, and a pardon is in process. Does that, as the American actor Clint Eastwood says, 'make your day?'"

"Thanks, Luis, I appreciate the information. Have you heard from Harv or the FBI man? I'd like to know my status in San Diego."

"Soon, Kile, very soon. Possibly today."

One of the English-speaking nurses entered and said, "Excuse me, gentlemen. Mr. Kile, there is a woman to see you, a Miz Cortland."

A vibrating silence echoed in Clay's ears. He glared at the nurse. She backed toward the door. Turning to Montoya, he asked, "Is this some kind of goddamned joke? If..."

"Her sister, Clayton. It must be. The one our people were to contact in Colorado. Remember?"

"Of course. I'm sorry, miss...*lo siento mucho*. Let's go. I never met her, Luis, so I have no idea what she's like."

The facial resemblance was startling. It would have been stronger except for the shoulder-length hair. She was waiting at the door. "Gwen? I'm Clayton Kile. Please," he motioned toward the room, "go on in."

"Thank you. She called you Clay, didn't she?"

"Yes."

"I'm Pamela, or Pam, not Gwen." They entered the room.

"My apology, Pamela," Kile said as he saw that two more of the six beds were occupied.

"Is there some place more private?" she asked.

"This is as private as it gets. Does that bother you?"

"Not really, they probably don't understand anyway. If I recall correctly, your relationship with my sister was not exactly an admirable one. You became a pest; that's the way she explained it once."

She doesn't seem particularly upset, Kile thought, but maybe it's a cover. "That was a long time ago. And I was more than a pest."

"What happened? Were you following her? The police said you two had been together for some time and that you'd been involved in some really bizarre things. But you had nothing to do with her death, according to them."

She was younger, as Kile remembered, two or three years. Was she shorter, or just heavier? "We met for the first time in years in La Paz. Quite by accident." Kile continued answering questions until the nurse's aide delivered the first lunches.

"I can arrange to have an extra tray brought in," Kile suggested.

"No, that won't be necessary. I'm meeting a friend for lunch—my traveling companion. He thought I shouldn't fly down here by myself."

"Will you come back this afternoon?"

"I don't know. You haven't told me...What I mean is, there's a lot more to this than you've told me, isn't there?"

Kile had left out a great deal: the cave, the lovemaking, and only in a cursory manner did he explain the fall and the kidnapping. "I didn't want to go over the grim details. Wasn't that covered by the police?"

"Yes, if you mean how she was killed. You haven't told me why you and Meliss stayed together through all this. It seems odd in view of the way she felt about you."

"I suppose we had a new understanding, perhaps I'd changed. I think we both had."

"One thing more, I get the impression you're some kind of hero. Why?"

"I'm not. I helped the authorities because of the identity thing mentioned before. Then when...when I heard about Meliss I got involved in the apprehension of the men responsible for her murder. That's all there is to it."

"I suppose it will drag on forever just like it does at home."

"That won't be the case at all. There will be no trials because they are all dead. It's over."

"Clay, I can't stay and I can't really talk now. I won't be back this afternoon."

"Have you arranged for burial, or will you be...?"

"She's already buried, Clay. I was on a raft trip going down the Colorado when the Mexican police called. There was no way of getting in touch. That's why I just got here. Can't see going through all the hassle and red tape so...well, let her rest where she is. Is this wrong? I'm buying a nice memorial stone."

"There's nothing wrong that I can see. She was headed for Chihuahua, you know. Do you need any money or some kind of assistance? I may be owed some favors."

"Everything has been arranged. Thanks anyway. Good-bye, Clay."

"Good-bye, Pamela. I appreciate your coming."

"You might drop by the cemetery when you're released. Maybe put some flowers out." She stood with the door open for several seconds. "I'm in the Denver phonebook."

"I'll remember." Kile felt something as the young woman left. What he was not sure. At least my emotional circuits aren't all burned out, he thought, as he adjusted the wheelchair to a table and removed the cover from his lunch.

In the afternoon Clarence Harvey and two men Kile had not seen before arrived. One was FBI, the other from the AG.

Kile was actually pleased to see Harv. "I was wondering when you'd come around," he said, offering his hand.

"Hear you did one hell of a job, Kile. We'll talk about that later. Right now, these gentlemen have priority."

The AG man advised Kile that he had been completely cleared by Dove's statements, but was needed for the prosecution of Trevis Thayne and his son. "Will you come voluntarily?" he asked. "We can't actually subpoena you from here."

"There are some matters pending," Kile said, "but of course I'll come when I can. Has a trial date been set?"

"Not yet, auditing has to be completed. That brings to mind one other matter."

"It does indeed," the special agent said. "The negotiable securities were returned, none missing. As to the currency, we are not sure. It is Heritage money, but we don't, at this point, know exactly how much you were given. Do you?"

"I wasn't given anything. They stuffed it into my briefcase without my knowledge. I never actually counted it." Kile explained that he used some of the money and would happily make restitution. "I know exactly how much I spent, and I am hardly indigent."

"There is another matter," the AG man said. "The savings and loan agencies and the court want you at the head of Heritage. At least until everything is unraveled, and that includes the money laundering thing. It may take a while. Interested?"

"Does the court know I am in custody, that I pled guilty to escape, and that I have killed several men?" There was a period of silence, then Kile added, "That might not inspire confidence in stockholders or investors, to say nothing of what defense lawyers might do on cross-examination."

The FBI man spoke first. "I see your point, but according to what Harv told me you are actually an agent of..."

Quickly interrupting, Harv said, "There are some fine questions of law here that I think should be reserved for the time being. There will be a full pardon from Mexico within the next day or two, and I think Kile's status as...well, as a legitimate officer of both the DEA and the Mexican government will be confirmed."

Somewhat flustered, the AG man said, "Perhaps we can use you as an investigative consultant, Mr. Kile, until all this is cleared up. I agree, there could be some problems."

"Okay for now, gentlemen," Harv interrupted. "Don't want to push, but I've got to get Kile down the hall. There are some loose ends to work out with Lieutenant Montoya. We can talk again this evening."

The loose ends turned into a full debriefing that lasted into the evening and began again the following morning. The next day Kile was transported to a closed judicial hearing. He was given a full pardon and sincere thanks from the government.

He was also admonished that any disclosures of the preceding occurrences and incidents were forbidden.

Two days later, with transportation arranged, Doctor Morello's authorization to travel, and the able assistance of Harv, Kile was ready to say good-bye to Luis Montoya.

"Got to make some last minute calls," Harv said, after wheeling him into Luis's room. "Back in ten."

"You never mentioned your conversation with the sister," Montoya said. "Is it a problem?"

"No. There is a strong resemblance, but she is not Meliss. It was difficult, not being able to tell her things I should have."

"Are you going to work with Heritage?"

"Yes, in one capacity or another. That is my profession, if you recall."

"Clay, that was your profession. You will never be content in that line of work, not anymore. My government is ready…"

"He's absolutely right," Harv said, as he burst through the door. "Things will be sopped pabulum, you'll see. Kile, goddamn it, my agency needs you. And, as I think Luis was about to say, his outfit wants you too. This whole goddamn thing isn't over by any means. We've only made a dent."

"Look, look at Montoya," Kile said. "Damn near lost his arm. I may have a limp the rest of my life. I've been through enough shit to last the rest of my life, and you idiots want me to join up on a permanent status? You're out of your minds."

"Okay, okay, but will you think about it?" Harv asked.

"Bored behind a desk? I'm going to love it. What do you guys pay anyway, half what I make? A quarter? You think I have some kind of death wish?"

"I give you a year, my friend," Montoya said.

"Hell," Harv added, "he won't last six months."

"And I was starting to like you, Clarence!"

"Glad I only have to get you to the airport."

There was a rap on the door. "*Entre*," Montoya said. "Ah, Captain Rosa, come in." The men shook hands as Rosa said,

"Some time off. Heard you were here and that you are now a lieutenant. Congratulations. And to you, Señor Kile, my warm greetings. You have been through a great deal."

A nurse entered. "Your taxi is here."

"Captain," Kile said, "it's good to see you. I'm sorry we can't visit. Luis Tlaxcala Montoya, I won't say it has been a pleasure, but it sure as hell hasn't been dull."

"*Adios, El Tiburón, y buena suerte*," Luis said.

Kile gripped the extended left hand, winked, then turned his wheelchair toward the door. "Let's go, Harv."

"A fine *gringo*, Lieutenant. What will he do, now?"

"I'm not sure."

"Will he come back?"

"Yes. One day he'll tire of high-heeled secretaries and business lunches. He will remember the Cortland woman and everything that happened. He'll find financial records and audits neither interesting nor exciting. People, for the most part, will be dull and not understand him. He's tasted a life completely foreign to him. What emerged from within changed him. For the first time in his life he really lived. Yes, Captain, he'll be back."